# CHRIS D'LACEY

# A CROWN OF DRAGONS

2 PALMER STREET, FROME, SOMERSET BA11 1DS

Text © Chris d'Lacey and Jay d'Lacey 2016

First published in Great Britain in 2016
Chicken House
2 Palmer Street
Frome, Somerset BA11 1DS
United Kingdom
www.chickenhousebooks.com

Chris d'Lacey has asserted his right under the Copyright, Designs
and Patents Act 1988 to be identified as the author of this work.

Cover and interior design by Steve Wells
Typeset by Dorchester Typesetting Group Ltd
Printed and bound in Great Britain by CPI Group (UK) Ltd, Croydon CR0 4YY

The paper used in this Chicken House book is made from
wood grown in sustainable forests.

1 3 5 7 9 10 8 6 4 2

British Library Cataloguing in Publication data available.

PB ISBN 978-1-909489-69-1
eISBN 978-1-909489-70-7

## ARTEFACT

**'THERE IS A QUESTION YOU HAVE NEVER ASKED ME, MICHAEL – ONE, I SUSPECT, YOU HAVE YET TO ASK YOURSELF.'**

We were sitting at a table in a windowless room, me and the android, Amadeus Klimt. The room was lit in mauve-coloured shades, though I couldn't see a light bulb of any description. We were somewhere within the UNICORNE complex – a craft of indeterminate size, laid deep underwater off the coastline where I lived, accessed through a complicated network of tunnels, hidden in the workings of a disused mine. They, UNICORNE, were an organisation that investigated UNexplained Incidents, Cryptic Occurrences and Relative Nontemporal Events. But the biggest mystery was

UNICORNE itself – the why, the what, and particularly the who, because the 'who' included my father, Thomas Malone, who had secretly worked for them before disappearing after a mission to New Mexico. Disappearing from family life, that is. For three long years, me, my mum and my sister, Josie, had suffered in silence, praying for news of Dad's return. Gradually, our hopes had dwindled to nothing. Then, shortly before my last birthday, along had come Amadeus Klimt to draw me into UNICORNE's clutches. An uneasy alliance that had culminated in the shocking discovery that Dad – or the shell of his body, at least – had actually been on this craft all the time, floating in a tank of gooey fluid, surrounded by small octopus-like creatures called Mleptra. And Klimt had the gall to say, 'There is a question you have never asked me, Michael.' Pick any one from a thousand, Mr Klimt. Starting with:

'Where's the nearest toilet?'

He tapped his perfect fingers on the table. 'This is not a moment for levity,' he said. He had a very slight German accent and an even slighter sense of humour. He levelled his purple-eyed gaze at me.

'I'm serious. I need to pee.'

'Interesting.'

'It won't be if I leak all over the floor. I thought you were bringing me here to show me an artefact?' After proving myself to them over two UFiles, both of which had almost got me killed, they had promised me 'a brush with dragons' and some answers about Dad – starting in what they called the artefact room.

'It appears you have already detected it,' he said. 'Or it has detected you. One of the most interesting phenomena associated with the scale is that its atoms vibrate at a rate somewhat higher than the coherent electromagnetic pulses that keep the rest of this planet stable. It is not uncommon to experience some discomfort around it.'

And that meant *what*, exactly? This was the way Klimt often spoke, like a physics teacher who'd got too close to his Van de Graaff generator. I crossed my legs and looked into a corner. The room was small, the walls just fading into shadow. Even the desk on which my elbows rested was as smooth as glass and completely black. 'Scale?' I said. It was the one bit of his sentence that had piqued my interest.

'Lay your hands flat.'

'Why?'

He tilted his head in a robotic manner, his standard way of expressing displeasure.

Sighing, I spread my fingers on the desk. The surface was slightly warm, not unlike the wall of the tank in which my father's body floated.

'A little wider, please.'

I moved my fingers until he told me to stop. 'Why am I doing this? What's going to happen?' He was scaring me now – something else he did on a regular basis.

Saying nothing, he swept one hand across the desk as if he was spreading a pack of cards. The surface cleared like mist off a window. And there, caught like an insect in amber, was the 'artefact' he'd brought me here to see. It was about the size of a man's hand and looked a little like a roof tile, longer than it was wide and gently furrowed from side to side. Its surface was rough, crusted with millions of tiny crystals, all glinting the same pale shade of green.

'You're not serious?' I said, even though just looking at the thing had registered a real wow factor in me (and, *boy*, did I want to pee).

'I assume,' he said, in as serious a tone as I'd ever heard him use, 'that you are asking me to verify that this is the object I sent your father to investigate in New Mexico?'

I looked at it again. 'Are you telling me this fell off a dragon?'

Another slight tilt of the head.

'But everybody knows that dragons aren't *real*.' I stared at the scale as if it was some kind of precious jewel, the most valuable thing in the entire world. Maybe it was. Maybe, deep down, I wanted to believe that this really had come from a dragon. Maybe this was the answer not just to where Dad was but to all those questions humans ask themselves from time to time. *Are we alone in the universe? What's our purpose? Why are we here?* Just thinking about it made my eyes water. It was a strangely emotional moment.

Klimt placed his hands flat on the surface of the desk and spread his artificial fingers like mine. What looked like a very fine lightning bolt emerged from the upper-most tip of the scale and skewered through the gooey stuff it rested in, before splitting and connecting to each of Klimt's fingertips. 'It does not matter how you name it,' he said. 'You merely have to accept that this piece of tissue – and I assure you it is organic – was once attached to a creature of some stature. Extensive chemical testing has established that it could not have come from a genus of dinosaur nor any reptilian, avian, or mammalian species known to have evolved on this planet. We call it dragon because we can find no better word for it. As you have frequently pointed out, a romantic mystique has formed around these creatures, but it would disappoint me if you bowed to such idle conjecture. You are, after all, a UNICORNE agent. Your role is to separate truth from fantasy. In this case, the truth is greater than the fantasy. To employ a term you regularly misuse, the scale is 'alien' to this world. How it arrived on our planet, we do not know. What happened to the creature that shed it is a mystery. But here it is. This is what your father brought out of New Mexico. This is what took him to the limits of human consciousness – and beyond.'

'This is what put him in that tank?'

He nodded. 'The Mleptra are keeping Thomas in biological stasis. But time is running out. He has grown weaker in the last two months. This is one of the reasons you are being activated.'

'Activated? What does—?'

'You have performed well for us, Michael, but your greatest test is still to come. I told you on the first occasion we met that you might be the only person capable of finding your father. The shell of his body may be in the tank, but his mind is elsewhere. We want you to find him. We want you to put him together again.'

Like all the king's horses in the nursery rhyme. If they couldn't manage it, why should I be able to? 'How?'

'Shortly, Preeve will prepare you for something your father called The New Mexico Phenomenon – or The Mexico Phenomenon for short. To perform this task, you will need to be connected to the scale at a high vibrational level.'

Preeve was their scientist, the man in control of the UNICORNE labs. He didn't like me much. To him, I was just an interfering little kid, someone he'd put in a jar if he could and screw the lid on tight. 'What is it – this . . . Mexico thing?'

'A means of accelerating your thought processes, allowing you to explore . . . deeper levels of consciousness.'

Why did I not like the sound of that? 'Will it be dangerous?'

'Do you really need to ask?'

That pee I'd been talking about? I thought I felt it as a warm patch on my thigh. It didn't help that a new bolt of energy had fizzed out of the scale and was connecting me to it in the same way as it had Klimt.

'Do not move your hands,' he said.

But it was hard to resist wanting to pull away. My fingers were beginning to tingle. It felt like the scale was scanning me somehow. 'What's happening? How is it doing that?'

Staring right into my eyes, Klimt said, 'The crystalline nature of the surface is home to thousands of Mleptra. They inhabit the minute cavities in and around the crystals as sea creatures would a shell. It is not clear how they survive, but they are extremely robust and highly adaptable to changes in their environment. As you know, we have extracted samples and found that they will grow in culture to the size you are more familiar with. The Mleptra have many remarkable properties, but they are probably little more than parasites. They cling to their host, this scale, not only because it offers them shelter but because they wish to absorb its power. Think back to what I asked you when we came into the room.'

'Something about . . . the question I've never asked?'

'Yes.'

I lifted my shoulders a touch. 'I don't know. I'm confused. What is it?'

'You have the power to alter your reality, to move away from dangerous situations by subtly reinventing the world around you. How many others do you know who are capable of that?'

'No one I've met.' Thank goodness the class idiot, Ryan Garvey, wasn't able to 'rearrange the multiverse' as Klimt liked to put it. We'd all be living in trees and eating nothing but popcorn if it was up to him.

'An incredible gift, you would agree?' said Klimt.

More often a curse than a gift. It had screwed up the life of my best friend, Freya, and turned her into a crow. But it had saved me from danger several times as well, and slowly – very slowly – I was beginning to learn how to master the reality shifts. I nodded. 'I guess.'

He smiled. A rare twist of the lips for him. 'But where did it come from, Michael? How did you acquire this extraordinary talent?'

'That's the question?'

'Yes.'

I shrugged again.

He looked down at the scale.

'*This?*'

He raised an eyebrow, another uncommon gesture for him. (It also made him look disturbingly human.) 'Look at your hands,' he said.

They were glowing green, the same colour as the scale. I could see right through the skin to the veins, where the blood was running a darker shade of green.

'Do you feel it?' he asked.

I jumped back, knocking my chair to the floor. After a few seconds, my hands returned to normal, but my heart was pumping like crazy. 'What have you done to me?'

'Shown you your place in the universe,' he said.

I shook my head and ran around the desk to the door. It was locked and wouldn't budge. I hammered my fist against it. 'Let me out!'

'And where would you go, Michael?'

'Home, to Mum. And this time I'm gonna tell her everything. *Everything.*'

'And she will think you delusional and bring you straight back to me.' He reached out and quickly gripped my wrist. I'd once been held by a chimp at a zoo after foolishly putting my hand into its cage. That chimp was strong, but nothing like as strong as Amadeus Klimt. 'An hour ago, in the director's presence, you were willing to go through any procedure that might enable us to contact your father. This is merely the beginning, Michael. If you fail now, there is no hope.' He let me go. I stepped away, clutching my wrist. 'I showed you the scale to uphold our veracity, but there is something else I want you to see, something that I hope will . . . secure your commitment to the mission.' He flipped his hand and a white rectangle lit up the wall to my left. A flickering ten-to-one count-down began, like an intro to an old-fashioned movie reel.

'What's this?'

'A film, made by your father.'

'What?'

'He's using an iris camera, a recording device secreted in a contact lens. A quite brilliant innovation, developed for us by Preeve. The images are jerky, but the eyecam has recorded documentary evidence of your father's time in New Mexico – seen, quite literally, through his eyes. Sit down, Michael. This is something you will not want to miss.'

And as a black hole formed in the centre of my chest, pulling everything I knew into its dark, tight grip, I sank into the chair again and stared at the screen.

## 2
## MONSTER
**· · · · · · · · · · ·**

**DAYTIME. THEY WERE TRAVELLING DOWN SOME WORN-OUT ROAD, DAD AND ANOTHER MAN, WHO WAS DRIVING (A JEEP, JUDGING BY THE** shape of the bonnet). For once, Klimt wasn't lying. My heart almost burst as Dad tilted his head, and the eyecam caught the reflection of his face in the side-view mirror. It was him for sure. His brown hair neat but fashionably long, his rugged face darkened by a day or two of stubble, those quick brown eyes piercing the lost years between us. My dad, Thomas Malone, alive. I put a hand across my mouth to hold back a sob.

'Where are they going?' I mumbled. The road ahead seemed pretty unending, a highway so straight you could have tipped your hat over your eyes and set the car on autopilot. A couple of times, Dad looked through his window, and the eyecam recorded a depressed desert landscape dusted with clusters of hardy green shrubs. In the distance, just topped by a ripple of cloud, was a backbone of snowcapped mountains.

'They are travelling south from a place called Carrizozo,' said Klimt, 'through a broad region known as the Chihuahuan Desert. The driver's name is Lynton. He is an archaeologist based at a nearby research facility.'

Appropriately, Dad looked across at Lynton. I couldn't see much of Lynton's face, thanks to the wraparound shades he was wearing. He had curly fair hair, tucked behind his ears in boyish waves. He looked about Dad's age, maybe younger. He said, 'We'll be leaving the highway at any moment. It's gonna get bumpy. The dig is close to the Three Rivers Petroglyph Site, but well outside the main tourist area. When we reach the camp, we'll need to do some walking.'

'I'm good with that,' said Dad. He had always kept himself super fit, a double for Indiana Jones, Mum called him. He said, 'Are there Mogollon petroglyphs at the site?'

'Mog what?' I looked at Klimt.

He held up a hand, suggesting I should watch.

'It was the glyphs that led us to the artefact,' said Lynton. 'There's a file beside you. Take a look.'

There was a rustle as Dad picked up a folder. The off-road bounce of the jeep made the film bob for a second or two. Then Dad was looking at a series of prints labelled

PETROGLYPH 1, PETROGLYPH 2 . . . They showed what you might call caveman drawings, simple shapes scratched on to rock – hands, weird faces, abstract symbols, horses, fish, the sun, the moon.

'Look at P-12,' Lynton said.

Dad shuffled the set. His eyecam settled on an image of a tall, round-shouldered figure with a head the shape of a regular light bulb, naked but for a cloth around his waist. His arms were like reeds, wavy, outstretched. Lines of light were pouring from his fingers into a universe littered with stars. Flying above him was a creature, unmistakeably a dragon. Flames were spitting from the dragon's mouth, making a crown of fire on top of the man's head. And in the centre of his chest, where his heart ought to be, was another, smaller, flame.

'Two cryptids in the same drawing,' Dad muttered. His thumb rubbed over the dragon shape. He had always liked dragons. One of the best gifts he'd ever given me was a paper chain he'd made of them. It hung on my bedpost to this very day.

'What's a cryptid?' I asked. For some reason, I felt the need to whisper.

'A creature unverified by the scientific community that is commonly believed to exist. Until your father came into contact with the scale, a dragon would have been a good example.'

I looked back at the film, in time to hear Lynton saying, 'Marie, one of the team, has more pictures on her tablet. The Mogollon Indians made thousands of drawings,

12

but we've never seen one like that before.'

'Any chance it could be fake?'

Dad's eyecam swung across the seats. He was trying to focus on Lynton's eyes, probably to use a technique called flecking. Dad could tell when people were lying by detecting minute changes of colour in their eyes. Green or red flecks were an indication of falseness. Gold was honesty. The driving angle combined with Lynton's shades meant it was impossible to see Lynton's eyes clearly, but his verbal response was pretty clear-cut.

'No,' he said, with a crispness that suggested he was peeved to think his expertise was being questioned.

Dad's hand, clutching a bottle of water, blanked out most of the shot for a second. 'So what do you make of the figure?'

The jeep bounced again, rattling every panel. It was a couple of seconds before Lynton responded. 'There's a myth about a monster that stalks these parts. A bipedal hominid, rumoured to stand up to ten feet tall. It's usually sighted in the Arizona pine forests, along the Mogollon Rim.'

'Arizona must be, what, a couple of hundred miles west?'

'More like three hundred,' Lynton corrected him. 'But the locals here all know the story. Ask any of them. Most believe in the creature. They say it takes the forest deer. Snaps the head right off before eating. Anyone looking at that image you're holding could be forgiven for thinking the beast is real.'

'This doesn't look like a monster,' said Dad. 'Super-human, perhaps, but not wild. What about the dragon?'

'That was the part we didn't understand – until we found the cairn.'

Dad shuffled the photographs again, bringing into the frame a picture of a mound built from hundreds of individual stones. A female archaeologist was standing beside it. The cairn was pyramid-shaped, a little taller than the woman. It didn't look like anything special, and Lynton seemed to agree at first. 'You see a lot of those in desert territories. They're mostly markers – navigational aids through snow and the like. But an isolated one usually indicates a burial place.'

'And this is where you found the artefact?'

The eyecam settled on Lynton again. He ignored the question and said, 'That's the camp up ahead.'

It was nothing much. A couple of tents in the distance.

'Listen,' Lynton went on, 'I need to tell you something. I know nothing about the people you work for or the chain of information that brought you here. I shared the news of this find with no one except Montgomery Humbel, my old professor. I'd trust Monty with my life. He's the one who arranged for you to come and investigate, but not everyone on the team is happy about having an outsider here. My principal colleague, Enrico Rodriguez, is suspicious of your motives. Rico has Mogollon ancestry. This find has left him pretty shaken. He wants the scale put back. He believes it was buried to protect the Mogollon. He thinks the figure in the petroglyph is a warning of what might come if we don't return the scale to its resting place.'

Dad glanced at the dragon petroglyph again. 'And what do you think?'

Lynton gave a nervous laugh. 'What I think doesn't matter. What I *know* is, we need to resolve this before we all dissolve into lunacy. I believe in dragons and ten-foot monsters as much as I believe the world is flat or that aliens regularly visit these parts, but there's something undeniably odd about this find. Since coming into contact with the scale, we've all been having vivid dreams or hallucinatory experiences.'

Dad allowed him a pause.

'I thought I saw my mother yesterday,' said Lynton, his knuckles white on the steering wheel. 'She was standing in the desert, a few feet from the tents, like she'd just grown out of the ground. She stared right at me, the hem of her dress flapping around her knees, white hair flowing freely in the wind.' The jeep bounced. Lynton swallowed hard. 'She's been dead for six years, Steve.'

'Your father was working under cover,' Klimt explained, 'using the name Stephen Dexter.'

The eyecam bobbed. Dad brought a photograph of the scale to the top of the pile. 'You've all handled it?'

'Minimally.'

'Where is it now?'

'Boxed, in the main tent.'

Dad nodded. 'Not everyone will share the opinion of Rodriguez. Surely you'd like to see the site fully excavated and the scale in a museum?'

Lynton drew a breath. 'If this . . . thing is what the Mogollon drawings suggest, it will blow the earth's natural history apart, and the theory of human evolution with it. I'd share a find like that with anyone who wants to see it. But this is New Mexico. Roswell territory. You've got Zone 16 just two states west. Every spook you've ever heard of has passed through here. If the wrong kind of people get hold of the scale, it will never see a museum, you can be certain of that.'

The jeep pulled up in an arc of dust.

'That's Marie,' said Lynton. Dad's eyecam settled on a youngish woman with straw-coloured hair tied up in a knot. She was wearing jeans and a battered green jacket, thick socks bunching out of her boots. She seemed disorientated, as if she'd had a knock on the head. She staggered towards the jeep.

'Something's wrong,' Lynton muttered. He jumped out and ran to meet her, leaving his door wide open.

Dad picked up a dog-eared safari hat, put it on, and stepped out of the jeep. He looked at Marie as she sank against Lynton. Fear had made dark hollows of her eyes.

Lynton lifted her face into the light. 'Marie? What's happened?'

'Rico,' she panted. 'Taken the scale. Gone into the desert.'

The eyecam panned the scene beyond the tents. There was no sign of anyone who might have been Rodriguez, just more parched plants and dead patches of ground.

'Where's Jacob?' said Lynton.

'Jacob Hartland is the fourth member of their team,' said Klimt.

Marie shook her head. She looked as if she might pass out at any moment. 'They got into an argument. Rico and Jacob. Rico went wild, shouting stuff about the Mogollon. He cut Jacob, here.' She ran a finger behind her right ear.

'Is he okay?'

'I don't know.'

'Look after her,' Lynton said. He handed her to Dad and sprinted to the tents.

Dad held Marie by the shoulders. 'Marie?' He shook her gently to make her look up. 'My name's Stephen Dexter. I'm here to help. How long ago did this happen?'

'Minutes,' she said, tears streaming down her face.

'Have you called anyone?'

She shook her head as she spoke. 'Wasn't *him*,' she muttered. 'Wasn't Rico. His eyes. It wasn't *him*.'

'Marie, look at me,' said Dad. 'Who was it? What did you see?'

'Monster,' she said, and collapsed into his arms.

# 3
## HOME
. . . . . . . . . .

**KLIMT STOPPED THE FILM THERE. 'SO, MICHAEL, HAVE YOU SEEN ENOUGH?'**

**ENOUGH? WHAT WAS HE TALKING ABOUT?** He'd only gone and left me on the worst cliffhanger EVER. I jumped up and touched my fingers to the screen. 'Of course I haven't seen ENOUGH! What happened next?'

'Hartland survived. He . . .'

'Not *Hartland* – well, I'm glad he was okay – but what happened to Dad? Did he go after Enrico or what?'

There was a silent beat. The room lights came up. Klimt put the dragon scale back into darkness. 'Read the file.'

He tapped a brown folder lying on the desk. Inside it was a top-secret file on my father, given to me by the

UNICORNE director, a scary character often referred to as the Bulldog. 'Why can't you just show me?'

'There is nothing more to show. Lynton called for medical assistance. While it was arriving, your father tracked Rodriguez into the desert, following directions to the cairn. It was dark by the time he found him. By then, the eyecam had failed.'

'Failed?'

'Completely. Preeve was extremely disappointed.'

He wasn't the only one. 'But Dad got the scale and you got him out, right? You told me you flew him home.'

'It is all in the file,' he said. 'You will find some interesting parallels with your own experiences. Now you will go. Your debriefing is over. Your mother is expecting you home tonight. We will contact you when Preeve is ready to begin your neural acceleration trials. It may be several days. A period at home will be good for you after the exertions of your last mission. We have, of course, arranged a diversionary story to explain your absence during the past two days.'

That made me snort. Combining the role of secret agent with regular schoolboy required a lot of 'diversionary stories'. 'What have you told her?'

'That you have been on an orienteering challenge.'

'*What?*'

'Agent Mulrooney's idea,' he said. 'He thought a mountain hike would be stimulating for you, after the recent difficulties you have had.'

Trust an ex-Marine to come up with that. I'd had a bad

car accident and a couple of school suspensions. Slogging over rain-swept hills with my head in a map was supposed to put me right, was it? 'And Mum believed you?'

'I am your doctor,' he said. 'Why wouldn't she believe me?'

Hmph. Easy for him to say. Hoodwinking Mum was a dangerous game. One of these days, we were going to trip up. And when we did . . . well, it didn't bear thinking about. I clutched the file double-handed to my chest.

Klimt spoke a command, and a computer somewhere clicked the door open. Agent Mulrooney was outside, waiting.

'Mulrooney will drive you home,' said Klimt. 'Enjoy the rest, Michael. Happy reading.'

Mum was her usual breezy self. 'Aha, the wanderer returns,' she said the moment I stepped into the kitchen at home.

'Um,' I grunted.

She shook her head and sighed in her *that's my boy* way. I'd been in the house for less than two seconds and already I'd gone from special agent to clueless boy-child. For once, I didn't mind. A normal family life was still the best antidote to my UNICORNE exploits, and often a source of comfort. My grunt was a timely reminder that I still wished to be Mum's beloved son, though I knew the response it would draw.

'So good to have you back,' she said. 'We miss his sparkling conversation, don't we, Josie?'

'Um?' said my sister. She had her head bent over her phone, texting.

'Never mind,' sighed Mum. 'Well, how was it?'

'How was what?'

She tutted. 'The great outdoors.'

Oh. Yeah. The orienteering.

'You *did* go walking?' she said.

'I was hoping they were going to tie him to a rock and see if he got struck by lightning,' said Josie.

I started with a hand gesture and thought better of it. 'It was good. Bit windy. No rain. The views of Holcombe Valley were exceptional.' (Mulrooney's words, not mine. He'd coached me on the drive home.)

'Oh, Holcombe Valley,' said Mum, drifting off. 'Me and your dad spent many a ...'

She trailed off, as she usually did when her fondest memories of Dad bubbled up.

'What's that?' she said, changing the subject. She nodded at the file. It felt like a ticking bomb under my arm. Given UNICORNE's top-secret status, it seemed odd they should entrust me with something so profoundly nondigital. One stumble and ...

'Homework,' I said.

Mum's nose immediately wrinkled. 'I wasn't aware the school was involved in this venture?'

'It's not school stuff, the Bull – Klimt gave it to me. Dr K gave it to me.' That was how she knew Klimt, as Dr K. 'Some geographical stuff he thought I might find interesting.'

'Well, don't let it get in the way of your schoolwork. You've got a lot of catching up to do, young man, after ... the word we do not mention.'

That word being *suspension*.

'Put any washing you have in the basket. You can tell us about your geographical adventures over tea.'

With a heading like CHIHUAHUAN DESERT, NEW MEXICO on the top sheet? No way.

For a full ten minutes, I sat on my bed with the folder closed beside me. It was as if I'd got a crucial exam result but was too nervous to open the envelope. I kept thinking back to my interview with Klimt, remembering things he'd said about the scale – and things he hadn't. If it *was* the source of my power to change reality, how had they used it on me? I'd always thought I'd inherited my abilities from Dad. Take the eye flecking thing, for instance. Klimt had told me I was able to do it because years ago I'd had leukaemia and Dad had saved my life by donating some of his bone marrow to me, passing on the flecking gift in his cells. But scanning flecks of colour was one thing; altering reality was in a whole different league.

I opened the file and turned the top sheet. It contained a detailed mission report, plus a transcript taken from a Dictaphone. It looked like a scientific journal, lots of tightly spaced lines of text. I desperately wanted to read it but was just too tired right then. So I put it aside and went downstairs, into the room that used to be Dad's study. Opposite the door was an alcove. In the alcove was a large oak desk. On the wall above the desk was a painting called *The Tree of Life*, by an artist named Gustav Klimt. Dad had been involved in the design and building of Klimt, the UNICORNE android version, and I was sure there was something about this picture that had influenced the project and caused Dad to name the android after the artist.

But what?

I let my gaze settle on the branches. They looked like you might imagine nerves to look, like the veins in my hand when I'd been connected to the dragon scale. As I held my focus, the picture seemed to change. The tree grew smaller, merging into a brain, then a forehead, then a face without eyes – the face of the Mogollon monster on the petroglyph.

'No,' I said, stepping away from it.

The monster widened its circular mouth.

'NO!' I screamed, falling with a thud against the door.

Somewhere just within earshot, I heard Mum saying, 'Michael?'

My heels dug into the carpet, my fingernails into the door.

A hollow sound came out of the monster's mouth, and with it just one word.

*Hartland.*

## 4
## MOMENT
· · · · · · · · · · ·

**THUD. *THUD*. MUM PUSHED AGAINST THE DOOR,
TRYING TO OPEN IT AGAINST MY WEIGHT.
  'MICHAEL, WHAT'S GOING ON?'**

There was panic in her voice. A tiny fear that was
always present, that she kept wrapped up in her constant
guise of brave single parent.

'Nothing,' I said, rolling away. I bundled myself on to
the edge of Dad's chair, laying my arms in an X across my
chest. I was shaking. Frightened. Sick to my stomach.
Wondering what the heck had just happened.

Mum rushed in and put a hand on my forehead. 'You're
freezing.'

'I'm all right.'

'You're not all right,' she said.

Josie appeared at the door. 'What's up?'

'Michael's got a chill.'

'Mum, I *haven't*.'

'Go and make him a hot water bottle, please.'

'For bed? It's only ten past five.'

'Josie, do as I say.'

'O-kaaay.'

Mum crouched in front of me, my hands in hers. 'Look at me.'

That was hard. I never could when she asked me to.

'Talk to me, Michael. What's the matter? I know something isn't right with you. I've known it for a long time.' She shook my hands. 'Why were you in here? Who were you shouting at?'

'That picture,' I said. 'I hate that picture.'

She glanced over her shoulder at *The Tree of Life*. 'Not crows again?' A reference to the solitary crow-like bird perched in the branches of the tree. My last mission had begun with Freya and crows. Freya. What I wouldn't have given to have *her* here now.

'No, it just . . . freaks me out.'

Her eyes narrowed. 'Okay, I get that – but why were you shouting?'

It's amazing how interesting carpets can be when you really don't want to talk to your mother. 'I thought I saw something.'

'What kind of something?'

'A face. I don't know.'

She drew in her lips. 'Was it your dad?'

'What? No-oo.'

'Who, then?'

I glanced at *The Tree of Life* again, thinking back to what Lynton had said about the dragon scale causing hallucinations. Was that why Klimt had exposed me to it, to see what effect it would have on me?

'You're tired,' Mum said, giving up on the questioning. 'And I don't mean hill-tired. All this business at school lately, I think it's been more stressful than any of us have imagined.'

'Maybe.' It was a feeble answer, but agreeing to something was easier than trying to avoid the truth.

She put her hand on my knee and rubbed it. 'Just tell me one thing. Why did you choose to come in here and look at the picture if you don't even like it?'

''Cause . . . *he* liked it,' I whispered, making it up as I went along. 'It makes me think about Dad.'

Her eyes began to look like dewy green grass. She picked up my hands again and kissed them, just as Josie walked in with the hot water bottle.

'Shall I put this in his bed, seeing as you two are having a "moment"?'

'No, I'll do it,' Mum said, breaking free. She dabbed the cusp of her eye with a tissue. 'The bed needs making, anyway.'

Josie held out the bottle as though it had suddenly turned radioactive.

Mum took it and left the room. To my surprise, Josie came and sat on the sofa. She started filing her nails. 'So what's bugging you this time, Freya or Dad?'

'Neither. It's that picture; it freaks me out.'

'It's just a picture,' she said.

I looked at the loudly patterned branches again. 'Really? It doesn't . . . mean anything to you?'

'Um . . . no?'

That was a relief. Literally days ago, this very picture had got Josie drawn into my last mission by mistake. UNICORNE had dealt with it by using an agent called Chantelle Perdot to selectively wipe out Josie's memories. Thankfully, it appeared to be working.

'Sorry, I'm being stupid.' I quickly changed the subject. 'Why're you doing that with your nails? Mum'll never let you paint them, you know.'

Josie examined one nail up close. She'd been paying more attention to her appearance lately; ten going on twenty-one, Mum said. 'I'm only *filing* them. What's it to you?'

Filing them.

Filing.

File.

DAD'S FILE!

Oh, my hairy aunt! I'd left it on my BED! And Mum was up there, sorting sheets!

I exploded from the chair and hammered up the stairs, crashing the bedroom door wide open.

Mum was there, a pillow under one arm, the UNICORNE file in her hands.

She was reading it.

'Mum, please give me that.' I held out a shaky hand.

She closed the file and put the pillow on the bed. She came to the door, all the secrets of Dad's New Mexico mission, there, in her grasp. 'Get into bed,' she said quietly.

'Mum, please give me the file,' I begged.

'No, I want to read it. All of it.'

I tried to snatch it from her.

'No,' she said firmly, holding it away. Her eyes drilled into mine. 'I'm going to read this, Michael. Now, get into bed.'

# 5
## BOYFRIEND
· · · · · · · · · ·

**I DIDN'T, OF COURSE. I DIDN'T GET INTO BED. I PACED THE ROOM LIKE SOMEONE HAD WOUND A SPRING IN MY BACK. WHAT TO DO? IN THE END,** there was only one option. I texted Chantelle, my first point of contact with UNICORNE. *Cover blown. Mum has info file on Dad. You need to get here NOW. You need to make her forget!!!!!*

It seemed like hours before she replied. *Don't panic. Will alert Klimt.*

I threw the phone down and sank on to the bed. Forget reality shifts, forget dragon scales; my world was about to turn inside out right here, in my room. What if Mum broke down? What if she couldn't cope with the truth? What if she never forgave me for deceiving her these past few months? What was she going to *find* in those pages? I didn't even know what was in the file, because I'd been too LAZY and too STUPID to read it.

AAARRGGGGHHHH!

I had to go downstairs and see her. I had to stand in front of my mother and say I was sorry, that Klimt and the Bulldog had sworn me to secrecy and—

The bedroom door opened. And there was Mum, the file held limply at her side. I looked into her big green eyes. No tears, just the slightest suggestion of wonder.

She said, 'Who else has seen this?'

She tapped the file against the frame of the door.

'Mum, I'm sorry. I'm really sorry.'

'Shush,' she said. 'It's all right. I'm not angry.' She came into the room and put the file on my desk, trailing her fingers across the folder. She hugged herself and walked over to the window. 'Seriously, have you shown it to anyone else – Mr Hambleton, for instance?'

Mr Hambleton? My English teacher? Why would I show it to—?

And then I got it.

OH MY GOD, she thought it was a story. She thought I'd invented a fictional file to explain Dad's disappearance to myself.

That crushing sensation of fear in my chest suddenly took a whole new random twist.

'N-no,' I said, barely able to squeeze the word out.

'Well, you should.' She moved closer to the window, looking but not looking at the view down the lane. 'It's very detailed. Very' – she sought a word – 'inspired. The way you've captured your father's voice is amazing. And that newspaper article is very convincing. How on earth did you make it look so real? If I was your English teacher, I'd be deeply impressed. You must have done a lot of geographical research.'

'Mum—?'

'I tried it once,' she went on, playing with an imaginary string of pearls. 'Writing, I mean, as a way of coping. I wrote a letter to Thomas on the anniversary of his disappearance. I told him everything that had happened to us over the year. How Josie had cracked a tooth at the swimming pool and you'd won your first chess tournament at school, how the car had broken down in the middle of town that time. Silly, really. It's still in a drawer somewhere' – she touched a hand to her lips – 'waiting to be posted.'

'Mum?'

Her head dropped and she started to cry.

'Mum, please don't.' I went over and stood behind her, raising my hands to the curves of her shoulders. I'd never reached out to hug her before. It had always been her who had comforted me. She felt so small as she turned.

'Oh, Michael. I miss him so much.' She laid her head against my shoulder, but only for a moment. 'I'm proud of you. I really am. This story, it's an incredible piece of work.'

'Mum—?'

'No, shush. I don't want you to apologise. I'm glad you've found an outlet for your feelings. This is your way of dealing with it, of letting go.'

*No*, I ached to tell her. *No, Mum, I'm not letting go. Just the opposite.*

'Did you have any help?'

'Help? What do you mean?'

'Did Dr K encourage you to do this?'

And what could I say to that? I was so desperate to tell her the truth, but what would be the point of hurting her further? Klimt was right; she'd just think me delusional. So I shrugged and said, 'He was involved, I s'pose.'

She nodded. 'He's a good man, Michael.'

I gritted my teeth and had to look away. Klimt, good? What's that expression people like to use? *The jury's still out on that one.*

'Hey, where've you gone?' Mum tugged my sweater.

'Nowhere. Just thinking.'

'Bad for you, thinking.' She smiled and put a hand flat against my chest. If I'd been wearing my school uniform, she'd have been straightening my tie for me now. 'Listen, there's something I want to tell you. I haven't said anything to Josie yet. I wanted to share this with you first.'

'Are you ill?' It sounded like that kind of speech.

'No,' she laughed. 'No, it's nothing like that. It's . . . well, there's no easy way to say this and there's never going to be an appropriate time, so I'm just going to come right out with it: someone has asked me out.'

'What, like a date? A *man*, you mean?'

'Yes, a man,' she said, doing her best not to smile.

'But you can't. You're married – to Dad.'

'I know.' She pressed her thumb against the back of her wedding ring.

'You just said you missed him!'

'I do,' she said. And now the smile had been replaced by a look of yearning. 'I miss your father more than words can say – but I miss having . . . company as well.'

'You've got me and Josie!'

'Yes,' she said, misting up again. 'That's true, I have. And you two are the best thing in the world. You really are. But it would be nice for me to have . . . a friend as well.'

'A *boyfriend*?'

'A friend,' she repeated.

'No,' I said, spinning away from her. 'No, you can't do this. Dad's still alive, I know he is.'

'Michael, please.' She glanced at the file.

On the bed, my phone buzzed. I saw Chantelle's avatar flash up on the screen. 'He's alive,' I repeated. 'And I'm going to find him and bring him home!'

Mum's shoulders sank. 'We'll talk about this another time,' she said quietly. 'I think you should get some rest.' And she stroked my arm and walked out of the room, leaving what felt like a huge void behind her.

I picked up the phone and read Chantelle's message.

*What is happening?*

I texted back. *All good. She thinks I wrote a story!*

Boyfriend. No way.

No one would ever replace my dad.

I couldn't let her do this. I couldn't allow Mum to give up hope.

Whatever it took, I would bring Dad home.

I tapped a final message back to Chantelle. *Tell Klimt I'm ready for TMP.*

My quest – my greatest UFile – had begun, and it had suddenly become more urgent than ever.

# 6
## SNAKE
· · · · · · · · · ·

**I READ THE FILE. I WASN'T GOING TO MAKE THE SAME MISTAKE TWICE. I'D HAD A MAJOR, MAJOR ESCAPE WITH MUM, BUT I NEEDED TO BE** sure now of what she'd seen. At some point, during some conversation, she was bound to mention the 'story'. And once Josie got wind of it, it would be all over school and her social media. If I said something too far out of context, they would pick me up on it right away. Then it might be hard to cover my tracks.

So I sat at my desk and revisited Dad in the Chihuahuan Desert. The first few pages mainly contained general information about his surroundings, the camp, the archaeology team, the injury to Hartland. *A gash like a small river,* Dad reported, running from the right ear down to the collarbone. It had missed the carotid artery but produced a significant amount of blood. The weapon was the scale itself.

Things got really interesting on page three. With the eyecam down, Dad had relayed everything into his phone. This was standard UNICORNE practice: record everything. A lot of it was boring stuff: times, dates, locations. But the active parts of the file read like the script of a spy novel, especially the part where he was tracking Rodriguez through the desert.

*Moving north-east at a steady pace. Difficult terrain. Ground still rising. Rockier now. Picking my way through boulder fields dusted with snow. Temperature okay, but night has fallen. Won't be long before the cold kicks in. Will have to abandon if – wait, I can hear something up ahead. Stones being moved. It must be Rodriguez. Yep, I see him. I see the cairn, by his light. I'm circling, looking for a better position. He's digging. Taking stones from the cairn. Talking to himself. He sounds . . . disturbed. I see a box that might contain the scale. Yes. He's just lifted the lid. Can't see the scale, but there's a glow from the box. Green. It's glowing green against the darkness, lighting his face. He's taken it out and rested it on his palms. Dropping to his knees – praying, I think. A language I'm not familiar with. Not Spanish. Something more indigenous. He looks wired. Doped, as if the scale has got to him. He's – jeez! What was that?! Something just flashed across the stones. Snake! It's a snake! It's gone for Rodriguez! He's been bitten. He's dropped the scale. He's rolling back in pain, clutching his thigh. He's crying out, grasping for a knife. I can see the snake clearly now, rearing, bold. Looks like a rattler, but its head is like nothing I've ever seen before . . . It's going to strike again. I'll never get to him in time. It's . . . Holy mother of mercy, it just blew FIRE from its jaws!*

'Dad, get out of there,' I found myself whispering. But he didn't, of course. He tried to help Enrico.

*Enrico is down. Not moving. I'm going closer. Don't think the snake has sensed me yet. Correction. It's turning. Its eyes, they're so . . . Damn, that was close! Just . . . able . . . to roll in time. Running for the cairn. Loose rocks there. Only chance is to — jeez, this thing's quick! That IS fire it's blowing. Repeat: fire, not venom. Got an idea. Climbing the cairn. It's weak on one side where the team has been digging. If I can coax this freak into the right position . . . Come on-nn . . . Come on-nn, you beast . . . Around this side. Just a little further . . . [sound of clattering rubble] That's it! I've got it! Top portion of the cairn collapsed with my weight. The snake's under the rubble, but it might not be finished. Checking Enrico. He's not breathing. No pulse. Eyes dilated. Burn marks on his chest. Smoking welts in the skin. I can't do anything for him. Retrieving the scale from among the rocks. Wow, this is something. Weighty. Crusted. Still glowing. Warm. Feels strange to hold it, as if it's probing me somehow, trying to connect. My heart rate's building. This is extraordinary. I've never felt anything like this in my life.*

'Dad,' I said again. 'Dad, get *out* of there.' I couldn't help running through the worst scenarios. What if the fire snake freed itself? What if Dad was overcome by the power of the scale? What if the Mogollon monster appeared?

And then something did appear.

*Lights*, Dad reported. *I see lights in the sky, panning the desert. Can't ID a chopper. No engine sound. Possibly military stealth craft. I'm moving away from the cairn. Will bury the scale with my watch if there's time, leave the GPS tracer on. [sound of scrabbling] That's it, I'm clear, but the craft is overhead. They've lit the cairn and Enrico's body. They'll find me soon. Nowhere to hide. Don't see a way out of this. I need to be a long, long way from here. If I could just – Uh! [sound of losing balance] Something . . . weird just happened. I'm . . . I'm still in the desert, but I don't know where. Don't recognise the mountain profile. I'm not by the cairn. Repeat: not by the cairn. It's as though a hand just picked me up and dropped me somewhere else. [sound of panting] Head spinning. Can't focus . . . Trying to stand . . . Can't . . . Can't . . . [sound of a body collapsing]*

The report ended there, with no further indication of what had happened. But I knew. Dad had experienced a reality shift, brought on by the scale. I turned the page. Pinned to the back of the transcript was another report with details of how UNICORNE had got him home. The sudden shift in his GPS position had made them send a drone to the new location. The drone had beamed back pictures of Dad lying on the ground in scrubland close to Highway 54. Two agents were sent to find him. The scale was put into an isolation vessel and eventually transported to UNICORNE headquarters via private plane.

The report said nothing more about Dad.

But a newspaper article at the back of the file did. It ran the headline: HERE BE DRAGONS? Underneath was a subheading: MOGOLLON MYSTERY AT THREE RIVERS.

Beside it was a picture of the 'monster' petroglyph.

I read the whole thing. It told the story of the petroglyph discovery and the alleged artefact found in the cairn, now missing. How there had been disagreements in the camp and Enrico had been found dead at the cairn. *The official autopsy result claims Rodriguez died from a snakebite, but there are persistent rumors of unnatural burn marks on his chest. And sources close to the story have suggested that his body contained high doses of radiation. So what did kill Enrico Rodriguez? And where is Stephen Dexter, the shadowy archeologist who reportedly followed him into the desert? No trace of Dexter has ever been found. His true identity remains a mystery. Was he planted there to steal the artifact, then airlifted out? If so, by whom? Was he captured and taken to Zone 16? Or is the truth stranger than we dare to imagine? Did whatever killed Rodriguez also abduct Dexter, taking evidence of the existence of dragons with it? What kind of monster really stalks the wastelands of southern New Mexico? We may never know.*

I sat back in my chair, tossing an imaginary basketball into a hoop. Reading the article had suddenly identified a whole new conundrum, one I'd never thought about till now. Since joining UNICORNE, I'd been so preoccupied with bringing Dad home that I'd never stopped to think about the implications of it. The questions in the press, for instance. *Where have you been, Thomas? Were you imprisoned? Why have you not come back or been released by now?* Dad's picture would be everywhere, the TV news, the papers, the internet. How long before someone began to speculate that Thomas Malone was Stephen Dexter, bogus archaeologist, Three Rivers thief? Come to think of it, why hadn't anyone thought of it three years ago? My heart skipped a beat. Maybe they had. Maybe Lynton and Marie were shown photographs of Dad but had both denied that he was Dexter. It wasn't difficult to see how UNICORNE could swing that. Lynton and Marie were dedicated archaeologists, and Lynton had even suggested on camera that he wouldn't want the scale in the hands of the government or Zone 16. I closed the file with a sinking feeling. Bringing Dad back might be the worst thing I could do for him. What hope would he have for a normal life? I picked up my paper chain of dragons. In my mind I plucked them like daisy petals. *He comes home, I let him go. He comes home, I let him go*. I didn't make it to the end of the chain. I didn't need to.

I knew their number was even.

# 7
## ATTIC
· · · · · · · · · ·

**I SLEPT SURPRISINGLY WELL THAT NIGHT BUT
WOKE EARLIER THAN NORMAL BECAUSE I
THOUGHT I HEARD SOMEONE TAPPING AT MY**
door. 'Josie, get lost,' I said into my pillow. But the sound
wasn't coming from the door; it was above me.

I rolled out of bed. Outside, the rain was pelting down.
Some had worked its way into the roof space, it seemed.
On the ceiling above my desk was a dull yellow stain.
Every few seconds came the *splap* of dripping water.
'Great,' I muttered, and got back into bed.

I told Mum at breakfast.

'Oh, no,' she groaned, and immediately ran upstairs to
look. She was back moments later with her phone to her
ear. 'Mr Grewitt? Yes, it's Darcy Malone. Havenhold

Cottage, on the outskirts of Holton? Yes, you pointed that wall for us last year. We've got a leak in the roof. Is there any chance . . . ? Oh, really? As long as that? Oh, dear. I don't think we can wait a week. I don't suppose there's anyone else you could—? . . . Oh, just a minute. I think we had a leaflet through the door from them.' She scrabbled through a box where we kept our telephone books and other bits of information. 'DH Roofing? They're okay, are they? I – yes, perhaps something temporary, until you can get here. Excellent. You'll call me? Or should I—? I will. Thank you so much. Thank you. Goodbye.'

She ended the call and quickly made another. 'Oh, hello. My name is Darcy Malone. We have a leak in our roof. I wonder if you could give me a call as soon as you possibly can, please. Thank you.'

She clicked the phone off and put the leaflet on the table.

'Dennis Handiman?' I said, reading it over my cereal bowl. 'You can't have someone called Dennis *Handiman* looking at our roof. You'll be having Postman Pat delivering our mail next.'

'If you've got any better suggestions,' she said, digging around in the cupboard under the sink, 'you're welcome to air them.' She plonked a bucket down in front of me.

'What's that for?'

'Cornflake challenge. I thought we'd fill it and see how long it takes you to eat a whole bucket load. What do you *think* it's for?' She dusted a hand over the top of my head. 'That walk across the hills was supposed to have blown the cobwebs out of your brain, not put it to sleep. You know how to operate the attic ladder. Go on. You'll be quicker than me.'

'You want *me* to go up into the attic?'

'No, I want you to lie on your bedroom floor with your mouth wide open in case any water falls through the ceiling! Just find the drip and put the bucket under it. And be careful where you put your feet. The space above your bedroom isn't boarded, so you might have to stand on the joists. On second thoughts, maybe I should—'

'I can do it.' I wrested the bucket from her. This would have been a task for Dad. Entrusting me with it made me feel like the man of the house. Besides, I'd never been in the attic.

'Oh, and give Josie a hurry-up, will you?'

I paused at the door. I was about to say something mean along the lines of *Am I allowed to kick her?* when I noticed Mum running what looked like lipstick around her mouth. She saw me looking and dropped the stick into her bag.

'It's a lip balm,' she said. 'My lips get chapped in the cold. I've used it for years. It's not what you're thinking.'

All the same, I couldn't help but make a dig. 'Maybe your boyfriend could fix the roof for us?'

'Don't,' she said, a tiny word that seemed to cover a multitude of larger possibilities.

She stared me right out of the door.

On the landing, near the bathroom, I bumped into Josie.

'What's that for?' She pointed at the bucket.

'Your head, because you're so ugly.'

'Wha——?' For someone who was actually very pretty, she had a scowl that could crack a lump of stone. 'You're pathetic,' she hissed. She stuck out her tongue and stomped downstairs.

She was right, I was pathetic. I shouldn't have been taking my anger out on her. But words like *I've got a lot on my mind* didn't really cut it with younger sisters.

The attic hatch was in the landing ceiling. Entry to it was a four-stage process:

• Using the pole stored in the airing cupboard, undo the hatch door and let it drop open.

• Hook the pole on to the last rung of the folding ladder.

• Draw the ladder down to floor level.

• Pick up thy bucket and climb.

A light came on the moment I poked my head through the hatch. The attic was bigger than I'd imagined, a wide open space with no walls, just lots of sturdy beams that crisscrossed where the house changed shape. It was cold up there, but no worse than the first frosty morning of autumn. There wasn't much to see: Josie's old dolls' house, two fake Christmas trees, an ironing board, a clapped-out oil heater and a stack of plastic storage boxes. The area around the hatch was boarded and therefore easy to walk on. I could stand up straight and touch the highest beams if I stretched. But Mum was right about my bedroom area. That was all open joists, running like railway tracks into the eaves.

I found the leak right away. There was a hole in the roofing felt, big enough to poke a finger through and scratch the tiles. Water was trickling through it, running down a rafter and dripping on to the insulating material that was stuffed between the joists like yellow candy floss. I knelt at the edge of the boarded area. I figured I could reach just far enough to place the bucket and catch the drip. But the bucket was unsteady on the insulation. So I crawled along two joists, using hands and knees, scraped some of the insulation aside, and put the bucket directly on to the ceiling plaster. It was still a bit lopsided, but it was catching the drip and it wasn't going to fall. Job done.

'Michael, how are you doing?' Mum's voice, from the landing.

'Okay!' I yelled back.

'Come on, then. We need to get you to school.'

School. That other essential ingredient of a secret agent's life. I wasn't a geek, but I did like school, especially English with Mr Hambleton. Everyone knew I was his favourite pupil, but he had to nudge me twice that day for staring out of the window. Even a stupid joke from Ryan Garvey couldn't get me out of myself. I couldn't stop thinking about Mum and the guy who'd asked her out. That moment when she'd touched my chest and said, *There's something I want to tell you* . . . ramped up the stress like nothing Klimt could ever throw at me.

I was still under a cloud when Mum came to pick up

me and Josie from school. I stared out of the window all the way home.

As we pulled into the drive, Josie said, 'Mum, there's a man on our roof.'

Dennis Handiman. His white van was in the drive.

Mum stopped the car and turned off the engine. It was still raining gently, but DH Roofing, to his credit, was indeed on the roof. Or rather, on a ladder, leaning over the roof. He was wearing tracksuit bottoms and a jacket so thick it could have insulated our hot water tank. On his head was what Mum called a trapper hat. One of those furry things with flaps over the ears.

'He called back, then?'

'Hmm, this afternoon. He asked me where the leak was and told me he'd pop by and have a look if he had time.'

'I'm going in,' said Josie. She shivered and got her keys out.

'You go, too,' Mum said to me. 'I'll deal with this.'

But I was interested to hear what Dennis had to say. After all, I'd been the hero of the hour this morning.

He waved and came down the ladder. In his hand was what looked like a broken tile. 'That's your culprit,' he said, striding up. He put two pieces of the tile together to demonstrate where it had cracked.

'Ugh, how did that happen?' Mum asked.

Dennis pointed at a nearby tree. 'Probably whacked by a branch in the storms.'

'Or a heavy foot,' Mum tutted.

'I haven't stepped on to the roof,' he said. A look of

46

concern lit his quick brown eyes. It was difficult to read much more of his expression, thanks to his dense black beard.

'No, no, not you.' Mum was quick to apologise. 'We had the TV aerial adjusted recently.'

'Did we?' This was news to me.

'Yes, while you were in hospital,' she said. 'I'm wondering if they were a bit clumsy up there.'

Dennis cupped his eyes and squinted at the chimney, where the aerial was fixed. 'I still favour the branch theory. Anyway, I've replaced the tile, but the one I've put up is a different colour. I can get you one the same as yours in a couple of days. Might be a good idea to renew the felt underneath it at the same time.'

'There's a hole in it,' I said.

'Yes, I spotted it,' said Dennis.

'Is that a lot of work?' said Mum.

'Not really. I'd need to take some rows of tiles off and cut and replace the felt. A quick check inside the roof space will show me the extent of it.'

'You'd better come in, then. Can I get you a cup of tea or anything?'

A smile broke through the beard. 'That would be great,' he said, though he sounded slightly hesitant. 'There you go, soldier. Souvenir for you.' He handed me the broken tile.

'That's actually strangely appropriate,' said Mum.

Dennis looked up for an explanation.

'He's writing a story about a dragon scale.' She tousled

my hair. MOTHER! I hated her doing that in front of strangers. I wasn't six any more. She was right, though, the tile did look a little like the scale in the UNICORNE artefact room.

'I, um, just need to get something from my van,' said Dennis, and was starting to drift that way when Josie shouted from the door, 'Mum, come quick!'

'Why, what's the matter?'

'There's a hole!'

'What hole? What are you talking about?'

'Oh, just come!'

'Excuse me,' Mum said, setting off for the house.

'This doesn't sound good,' said Dennis. He looked me up and down for a moment. 'Go on, you lead. I'll get what I need and follow you in.'

I nodded and hurried inside.

'Oh my goodness!' I heard Mum cry.

I pounded up the stairs.

They were in my room. There was a hole in the ceiling. On the floor beneath the hole was an upturned bucket and a mound of plaster. A great plume of dust was hanging in the room.

'Ohhh, dear,' said a voice from the landing. Dennis put a reassuring hand on Mum's shoulder. 'It's a mess, I know, but it can be fixed.'

Josie turned away, shaking in horror. 'Whose head is that bucket for now?' she hissed, and waltzed off to her room.

# 8
# PACKAGE

**MUM RARELY GOT FLUSTERED, BUT SHE WAS IN A STATE NOW. 'RIGHT,' SHE SAID, 'WE'RE GOING TO NEED BAGS AND . . . AND TOWELS TO DRY THE** carpet. And the curtains will have to come down. Oh my goodness, this dust is *everywhere*. I'll have to call . . . I think the insurance documents are in . . .'

'Can I make a suggestion?' Dennis said calmly.

Mum put her fingers to her temples. 'Please do.'

He stepped into the bedroom and looked at the hole. 'Before you do anything else, we need to tidy that up to make sure no more plaster comes down.' He picked up a piece that had landed on the floor. 'This stuff's heavy. It'll give you a nasty headache if it drops. You'll need proper rubble bags for the mess.' He dipped into his pocket for a set of keys and threw them to me. 'Blue bags. Back of the van. Bring them all. Do you have a pair of stepladders?'

'I'll get them.' I put the broken tile just inside my room.

Mum shook her head. 'You're getting the bags.'

'I can get the ladders on the way back. They're only in—'

'Michael, just—' She broke off, squeezing her fingers into fists of frustration. She would never have blamed me directly for what had happened, but this was hard for her all the same. She loved this house. I could see she was already thinking ahead, wondering how we would cope with my bedroom out of action. The clean-up. The carpeting. The redecoration.

Once again, Dennis came to my rescue. 'Got an old sweater and jeans, Michael?'

'Um, yeah.'

'No,' said Mum, realising where this was going.

Dennis stuffed his hands into his pockets. 'His bucket, right?'

Mum took a breath.

Dennis said to me, 'What do you normally do while your mum's cooking tea?'

I shrugged. 'Homework?'

'In here?'

'Yes.'

'Well, tonight you'll learn something about the building trade. In the van you'll find some big dust sheets.

Bring one of those as well.'

Mum folded her arms. 'Look, this is very good of you, Mr Handiman—'

'Dennis,' he said.

'But . . . we're taking up your time. And we need to discuss . . . a price for the work.'

He looked at me again. 'Cup of tea was mentioned, wasn't it?'

I smiled. I didn't drink much tea.

'I meant for replacing the tile,' Mum said.

He raised a hand. 'It took two minutes. Look, we can sort out money after I've secured this hole. Then you can decide how you want to proceed.'

He sent me away with his eyes.

When I returned, with bags and sheet and stepladders in tow, Dennis had worked some kind of magic on Mum. She had gone downstairs but left some old clothes on the floor outside the bedroom. By the time I'd changed out of my uniform, Dennis had bagged up the biggest bits of plaster and was arranging the stepladders under the hole. 'Spread the sheet out on the landing,' he said. 'Two important rules of the trade: try not to make the mess worse, and always clean up after yourself.'

I spread the sheet and came back in.

He was already at the top of the ladders. 'I'm going to break off some loose chunks. You hold a bag open and I'll drop them in, okay?'

'Okay.' I grabbed a bag.

'We need to get back to sound plaster. It's an old ceiling,

but it's not in bad shape. Once these loose bits are off, it should hold. The water will have weakened it. If you ever need to catch a leak up there again, put a board across the joists and the bucket on the board, okay?'

'Yeah,' I sighed.

He snapped off a piece of plaster. 'Stuff happens, Michael. Don't beat yourself up.' He dropped the chunk into the bag. 'So, dragons. You keen on them?'

'Kind of, yeah.' My gaze flashed to the bed. In all the fuss, I'd forgotten about the folder. I'd left it out because Mum had already seen it and Josie wouldn't come into my room for any reason. But I didn't want an outsider to open it. Right now, it was covered in plaster dust. Untouched.

'My girl loves dragons,' he said, dropping another chunk.

My arms sagged. He was right, the plaster was heavy. 'You've got a kid?'

'Melody. Bright as a button. Crazy about unicorns and dragons. What's the story you're writing?'

'Oh, nothing.' Again, I flashed a glance at the file. Was he probing or just making conversation? The mention of unicorns was particularly unsettling. If there was one thing Agent Mulrooney had taught me, it was always to be on my guard.

'Melody's favourite bedtime story is about a dragon that drops its scales in the autumn—'

*Thud.* The next piece of plaster hit the bedroom floor.

'A bit like that. I thought you were under it.'

'Sorry. It's just . . . Can we talk about something else?'

'Sure.' He broke off a smaller piece of ceiling, making sure it went into the bag. 'What time does your dad get home?'

'All right, who are you?' I put the rubble bag down.

'What?' The hat flaps hugged his puzzled expression.

'Who sent you?'

He looked away for a moment. 'I'm a roofer, Michael. I work for myself.' He came down and grabbed an empty bag. 'Look, I'm not sure what I've done to upset you, but I can manage this on my own. Go and see your mum. Tell her I'll be another few minutes. Then I'm out of your hair, okay?'

I looked into his eyes and saw flecks of gold. He was telling the truth, and now I'd made myself look totally stupid. 'I'm sorry. It's just . . . my dad doesn't live with us any more. He liked dragons. Sensitive subject.' I picked up the paper chain looped around my bedpost. Thankfully, it hadn't been damaged.

He glanced at it and said, 'Well, that's cleared the air – in a manner of speaking.' He waved some plaster dust away from his face. 'Shall we finish the job?'

'Okay.'

He handed me the empty bag. 'There's only one bit left.' He pointed to an area where the plaster was cracked.

We took up position again and worked in silence for a few seconds. Then he said, 'So, at the risk of you kicking my stepladders over, what do you think of Manchester United's chances this weekend?'

'Oh, I'm not a football fan,' I said.

'Fair enough. Any hobbies?'

Solving murders, visiting ghosts, talking to crows, flipping reality. Nothing too exciting. 'I like riding my bike.'

'Neat. What make have you got?'

'Nothing special – but it's new. I got it for my birthday.'

'I love cycling,' he said. 'Do you all go out?'

'We used to, when . . .' I dropped my gaze. We used to go out when Dad was around. Even Mum had her own bike then. I hadn't thought about that for ages.

'Hello, what's this?' Dennis said.

I looked up. In his left hand, he was holding a lump of plaster, but with his right he was tugging at a piece of plastic. He pulled down a sealed polythene bag. There was a small brown envelope inside it. 'It was underneath the insulation.'

'Hidden?'

'You tell me.' He shrugged and stepped down off the ladders. He took the bag from me and put it with the rest. 'I'll be downstairs, chatting with your mum.'

'Dennis?'

'Yes?' He didn't turn around.

'Don't say anything to Mum – about this.'

He took off his hat and dusted it down. He had black cropped hair, the same black as his beard. Somehow he looked taller without the hat. 'I fix things in people's houses, Michael. What I see of their lives is none of my business. You want to make your mum happy?'

I nodded.

He bent down and picked up a small piece of plaster. 'Then do what good kids are s'posed to do: don't make problems for her – and tidy your room.'

# 9
## DVD
· · · · · · · · · ·

**I OPENED THE BAG AS SOON AS DENNIS HAD
GONE. THERE WAS NO WRITING ON THE ENVE-
LOPE, AND NOTHING TO INDICATE WHO IT MIGHT**
be for or who had put it in the attic – though I assumed it
must be Dad. In the envelope was a small DVD, half the
normal diameter. The words *Day 4* had been written
across it in black felt pen. I wasn't sure a disc of this size
would play on my computer, but I couldn't risk starting
my machine in this dust cloud. So I retrieved the file on
Dad, cleaned the mess off it, put the disc in its envelope
inside the folder, and hid the folder under a batch of
towels in the airing cupboard.

Then I started to clean up.

Five minutes in, I realised it was hopeless. The room

needed to be stripped, and I was floundering without Mum's guidance. So I picked up what I could of the smaller bits of plaster, bagged them and went downstairs.

Josie was in the front room, watching TV. Mum and Dennis were in the kitchen, talking.

'That's what I'd do,' I heard Dennis say.

'What?' I said, coming in. 'What would you do?'

He was sitting at the kitchen table, hands around a mug of tea. He looked at me a little anxiously, I thought. 'False ceiling. We screw battens to your existing joists, pop on some plasterboard and skim it. Job done.'

'Will we need to clear the room?' Mum asked.

He shook his head. 'No, I'll cover everything. Might have to shift some furniture around, but I'll cope.'

'So there's no point in tidying, really?' I said.

Dennis laughed. 'This kid is sharp.'

'Hmm.' Mum raised an eyebrow. 'The most pressing question is, where is Michael going to sleep while all this is happening?'

'He's not sharing with me!' cried a voice from the front room.

Dennis walked to the sink, washed his mug and put it on the drainer. 'Can't help you with that one, I'm afraid. I'd better be off. I'll see myself out. I'll be in touch to sort out a timetable for the work.'

'Thank you so much,' said Mum.

She touched his arm.

He made a calling sign with his hand, glanced at me briefly, and left.

'Right,' said Mum, as the front door closed. 'We need to get some clothes from your wardrobe and any other odds and ends you need. What's the matter? Why are you looking at me like that?'

'You touched his arm.'

'So?'

'And I saw the look you gave him when he washed his mug.'

'I appreciate politeness,' she said starchily.

'I think he's handsome,' Josie said, overhearing.

Mum threw down a tea towel. 'See what you've started?'

I scowled and sank back against the fridge. 'Where *am* I going to sleep?'

'Holton Woods, if you're not careful.'

'Good idea, Mum. Maybe the squirrels will eat him!'

'Josie, shut up,' she said. 'It will have to be the air bed in the study. Are you going to be okay with that? We can take the picture down if it bothers you.'

I shook my head. 'It'll be all right. Can I take the laptop in?'

'Yes, but not now. Your tea's almost ready.'

Typical. There I was on the brink of what might be an amazing discovery, only to be thwarted by a plate of fish fingers.

Still, an agent had to eat.

After the meal, the relocation started. Mum changed into some old clothes and together we emptied my wardrobe and drawers. She moved some non-essential clothing into her room but stacked the everyday items like socks and T-shirts on the sofa in the study, telling me to keep it all neat. *Um . . .*

'We'll leave the desk clear for you to work on,' she said. 'We could bring your computer down if you like, though I wouldn't trust that keyboard. It was pretty thick with dust.'

'I'll just use the laptop,' I said. You could fold a laptop in under a second. Very useful for keeping nosy sisters at bay.

Finally came the air bed. We inflated it using the pump that came with it. Mum made me lie down on it to check that it was okay. 'It won't be for long,' she said, noting my faraway expression.

But I wasn't thinking about the inconvenience. I said, 'Weird to think that the last person who slept on the air bed was one of Josie's friends.' That 'friend' had actually been Freya, disguised as a girl called Devon Winters. A clever ruse to keep her close to me during my last mission – when she could still be a girl.

'Well, I'm sure you won't catch anything,' Mum said.

No? I felt my neck, where there was still a scar, made by Freya's crow claws. That made me think about the archaeologist Hartland, and that strange incident with the *Tree of Life* picture. I really had to talk to Klimt about that.

'Right, you'll need some bedding,' Mum said. 'There's a spare duvet and pillows in the airing cupboard.'

'I'll get them!' I sat up as if I'd been struck by a bolt of lightning.

'Don't be silly,' she said. 'The airing cupboard is a

complete mystery to you. The only time you've ever looked in there is on that Easter egg hunt we did once.'

When the chocolate had melted on the towels. Yeah.

I jumped up and walked past her. 'I'll get my own bedding. You'll only bring a duvet cover with roses on or something.'

'Fine,' she said, throwing up her hands. 'Honestly, the older you get, the more I struggle to figure you out.'

'That's 'cause boys are super intelligent, Mum.'

'Of course. Silly me. I was forgetting that. Make sure you bring a single, okay?'

'Single what?'

'Single duvet, Michael.'

I raised my shoulders. 'I'm only gonna need one.'

She ticked the air. 'And the point goes to Mrs Malone.' Duh?

I went for the stuff. I brought the folder down with it, wrapped in the duvet. Before Mum came in to make up the air bed, I slipped the folder into the desk drawer.

And then I waited – until they had both gone to bed. I gave Mum another half-hour to nod off, then grabbed the laptop from the front room and started it up on Dad's desk. I put the DVD in the slot. Some sort of media software opened a window in the centre of the screen, and a file started to auto-play. The picture resolution and the sound were both shaky, as if someone had used a mobile phone to secretly record the images I was seeing. And what images. Dad, slumped in a high-backed chair, his face lightly bearded, eyes closed.

'Where are you?' a voice asked him. A voice I recognised. Liam Nolan, Dad's old doctor. A man who had shady connections to UNICORNE.

Dad rolled his head to one side. He looked hypnotised – or drugged.

'Where are you?' Nolan asked again gently.

'Mountains . . .' Dad murmured, but it wasn't his voice. He sounded young, like a boy. And his accent was strange.

'What do you see?' asked Nolan.

Dad suddenly opened his eyes. They were huge and staring, as if he'd seen something wild in the distance. 'Pa!' he yelled. 'Pa, they're comin'!'

'Ask him what's coming,' said a deeper, gruffer voice. The Bulldog, I was sure of it. So they weren't in Nolan's surgery, more likely on the UNICORNE craft.

Dad started breathing fast. For some reason, he stared all along his left arm. I thought I saw his skin turning green and scaly. And then he said the weirdest thing I'd ever heard, in a voice so low it made the speakers shudder. '*Galan aug scieth . . .*'

He put his head forwards and roared.

There the film ended, with Dad's face twisted like some kind of demon's.

And fire emerging from his left hand.

# 10
## HUMILIATION

**I MUST HAVE WATCHED IT FORTY OR FIFTY TIMES. ESPECIALLY THE LAST FEW SECONDS. I TRIED TO FREEZE IT OR RUN THE END IN SLOW** motion, but the software wouldn't allow it. None of this made any sense. I'd seen Dad's body, in a tank of fluid. I hadn't paid close attention to details, but I didn't remember that his hand was disfigured or that there was anything wrong with his arm. Maybe the octopus creatures, the Mleptra, had cured his injuries? Or maybe I was mistaken about the fire? The longer I looked at the film, the less convinced I was of what I'd seen. The final images were scratchy, and someone had knocked a light across the camera as people rushed forward to restrain Dad. Maybe it was nothing but a flare of light? How could a man make fire in his hand?

Then again, how could a snake breathe fire from its jaws?

I googled the phrase he'd used. *Galan aug scieth.* I tried every translation tool the internet could offer. No language software recognised those words. And who had Dad been shouting to? Who was Pa? When I ran those sequences again, he didn't seem to be talking to anyone in the room. He was looking way above their heads, as if he was seeing something in the sky. It reminded me of the time we'd run up Begworth Tor together to get the best view of an aerial display team called the Green Arrows. I was first to the top. I'd seen the lead plane and shouted back: *Come on, Dad! Quick! I can see them! I can see them!* All the time my eyes were trained forwards and up. So what was Dad seeing if it wasn't planes? Only one answer came to mind.

Dragons.


Mum found me in the morning, slumped over the laptop. I'd fallen asleep at the desk.

'Oh, Michael!' she huffed, shaking me awake. 'What have you been doing all night?'

The film! If she saw it, she'd totally freak out. Fortunately, the screen was blank. The laptop had gone into hibernation.

'Sorry. I was trying to catch up with homework.'

That took the edge off a little. 'Well, go and take a shower. You've been in those sweaty old clothes all night.

I'm not having you sent home from school because no one will sit near you.'

And she left me to it.

I moved to eject the DVD, then had an idea. Quickly, I grabbed my phone, made a wireless connection to the laptop, and downloaded the movie on to the phone. Then I put the DVD back inside the file folder and hid both among Dad's stack of old vinyl albums. You could have hidden nuclear alarm codes there; no one ever messed with those albums.

School that day was even more of a blur. I got another warning, in chemistry this time, for letting a flask of copper sulphate boil dry. I couldn't help it. I just couldn't concentrate on my classes. All sorts of problems were nagging at me now, especially that DVD. When exactly was it put into the attic? At first I thought it might have been *before* Dad went on his mission to New Mexico. But his appearance told me that couldn't be right. In all the years I'd known him, he'd never grown facial hair. So the *Day 4* film was shot *after* he was brought home from New Mexico, during that murky window of time between the moment he was rescued and the point when his body had been put into the tank. What exactly had happened then? How had Dad gone from a normal human being to a specimen suspended in a very big jar? Klimt had talked about quarantine, but Dad must have been active for a while when he returned, and yet he'd been declared as missing. Why? This still didn't answer the DVD question, or the bigger question that accompanied it. Never mind *when* the disc was put into the attic. WHO was responsible for putting it there?

I could think of only two possibilities. Top of the list was the UNICORNE agent Mulrooney. He was well trained in covert activities. Not long ago, Klimt had sent him to break into the house to plant a false note (allegedly from Dad) for me to find – a lure to take me to Liam Nolan, whom they suspected of leaking information to a journalist called Candy Streetham. Liam Nolan. Again. It wasn't inconceivable that Mulrooney had gone into the attic and planted the DVD at the same time he'd left the note – but why? Why would Klimt instruct him to do that? And when did Klimt expect me to *find* it? Now? A year later? Twenty years later? It didn't make sense. And despite the break-in, I trusted Mulrooney. Yes, he was a dedicated UNICORNE agent. But he had a heart. He cared about me. Unlike his fickle comrade, Chantelle, who seemed to be as changeable as the wind. Her heart, I was sure, was chiselled from ice.

There was only one other suspect: the man who'd fixed the TV aerial. Years ago, I remembered Dad messing about up there, redirecting cables – into his study of all places – so we could have a spare TV. Maybe the aerial man had wanted to 'check' the cables? A quick word with Mum would soon establish whether he'd been in the attic or not. But if that was right, who was he? And how did he get the film? And why would he leave it in such a strange place? And who was he working for? And—?

'Hey, Malone, you loser! Kick the ball back!'

It was lunchtime, and I was on the playing fields.

'Look at him,' I heard someone mutter. 'He's like that . . . daffodils guy that Hambleton's always going on about.'

'What?'

'You know. That poet. Wandering around on his own, like a cloud.'

'You're mental. Malone. KICK the BALL back!'

I looked up to see Ryan Garvey pointing at a football that had rolled to my feet. Without giving it much thought, I swung my foot and punted the ball to him. That was the intention, anyway. The ball sliced to my right and sailed over some railings, into a locked compound by the school kitchens, home to a bunch of large skips.

'Oh, no!' the football players groaned.

'Right, get him!' said Garvey.

They came for me like a pack of dogs.

'I'll get it! I'll get the ball!' I protested.

'Yeah, minus your trousers,' someone said.

Within seconds, they had me off the ground, my waistband unbuttoned and my zip undone. I was just about to face the worst humiliation ever when two fierce cries broke up the laughter.

*Ark! Ark!*

The gang dropped me in an instant. Everyone shrank away, covering their faces. I stood up, grabbing my waistband, and saw two crows circling overhead. A third crow landed on my shoulder.

'In trouble again?' it rasped in crowspeak.

'Freya,' I whispered. I couldn't help but smile.

'I trust you missed me, Michael?'

So much.

And while the football players looked on open-mouthed, I re-zipped my trousers and walked away with my best friend in tow.

# 11
# ENIGMA

**JUST SO I WOULDN'T LOOK TOTALLY WEIRD, I SAID 'TREE STUMP' TO FREYA AND JOLTED MY ARM. SHE FLEW OFF, WHEELING OUT OF SIGHT** beyond the trees at the far side of the football pitch. By the time I'd got there and sat on a stump where a companion tree had once stood (and where, poignantly, she and I had first talked), she had worked her way through the branches and was perched above me, just out of sight.

'Can I speak normally?' I whispered.

She made a sound like a nail being scraped through grit. My ability to speak in the crow tongue was patchy. Most crow-to-crow talk was a mixture of rasps and tail flicks and posturing, but because Freya had once been human, she could still recognise everything I said to her. She preferred me to speak as she did – *Ark!* – but when time was short, it was easier and quicker just to let me ramble.

'Got a lot to tell you.'

*Ark!* Then say it.

So I told her everything, picking up from the moment she and I had parted at the end of my last mission, the 'debriefing' session with Klimt, and everything I now knew about my father.

'He's alive?' she grated.

'If you can call it that. They've got him preserved in a tank of fluid. He's in a kind of coma. His body's okay but his mind's . . . not there. Klimt says the Mleptra are keeping Dad going – but he says Dad's getting weaker as well. So they're stepping things up. They say I'm ready for this thing they call The Mexico Phenomenon.'

*Ark!* That seemed to annoy her.

'I know you think it's crazy, but they say I can bring Dad back. I have to try it, Freya.'

'Film,' she caarked. 'Show me.'

I took out my phone and ran the clip. She tipped her head as she watched it, the images flickering in the curve of her eye.

'Do you know what he's saying? *Galan aug scieth?*'

She opened her beak and repeated the phrase. *Ark!* she grated after a while. No.

I sighed and clamped my hands to my head. 'What did they do to him, Freya? He looks more or less normal on the DVD. How did he get from that chair to the tank?'

'They know.'

'Who, Klimt and the Bulldog? Of course they—'

'The one who placed the disc. They know.'

'But I don't know who that is.'

The first bell rang for the end of lunch.

'We will watch,' said Freya. 'The crows will watch.'

'Watch who?'

'You. The house. Everyone.'

I nodded. 'I'll find out who the TV repair man was.'

*Ark!*

'Freya?'

*Ark?*

I touched the side of my neck, feeling the scar she'd left me with. 'Klimt says they cured me of the crow virus. I can't transform any more. I'll never be able to fly with you again.'

She gave me one of those broody stares that only a crow knows how to deliver. Then she opened her beak as wide as it would go and let out a cry that rattled my eardrums long after she'd taken off.

The second bell rang.

Shoot! I leapt up and sprinted across the playing fields. I burst into Mr Hambleton's room two minutes later – two minutes late.

'Michael,' he said. 'And to what do I owe the pleasure of your company?' Kids laughed. Kids way older than me. Oh, no! I'd run to the wrong class!

By the time I'd made it to the right class – Mr Greenway's

biology lesson – I was seriously late. 'Afternoon detention,' he said without fuss. 'The whole of your break time
in here, studying. Take your place, please.'

'Yes, sir,' I sighed, dragging myself to the bench where I
sat. On it lay a folded piece of paper. I opened it to find a
terrible drawing of my face on a crow's body. Ryan made
an L shape with his hand and stuck it to his forehead. Fair
comment. Every time I thought I was getting somewhere
with Dad, a zillion other puzzling questions cropped up. I
felt like a loser right now.

Break time followed the lesson. I stayed where I was
when everyone else left, waiting to see what Greenway
had in store for me. He wasn't a harsh teacher, so I knew
it would be mild. He came over with a textbook.

'I'm hesitant to believe this, as it came from Garvey's
lips, but he says you picked up a *crow* on the playing
fields?'

'Sort of.'

He tutted (at what he thought was my stupidity, I
guessed). 'You really are an enigma,' he said, as if I'd been
discussed at length in the staff room. 'Right, well, read and
absorb this passage, pages 170 to 175. It will give you
plenty of information about the most common types of
*Corvidae*. I'll be asking questions afterwards. So don't
think you can just go to sleep for twenty minutes.'

He put the book in front of me.

It was tedious, but I read it. I scored four out of five
correct answers to his questions. Satisfied, he told me I

could go. But as I picked up my bag, for some reason I asked, 'Sir, do you know anything about dragons?'

'Not really part of the syllabus, Michael.'

'They were birds, though, weren't they – kind of?'

'Well, if you take the line that dragons are really dinosaurs misinterpreted, then yes, they might be classed as avian. The latest line of research seems to indicate that birds are the closest living relatives of dinosaurs. Odd subject for a Tuesday afternoon.'

'Do you think they were ever real, sir?'

He rested his fists on his desk, gorilla-style. 'Are you mocking me, Michael?'

'No, sir. I'm just interested in why people think that dragons might have lived.'

'Well, that's more of a psychological question than a biological one, isn't it? Personally, I lump dragons in with aliens and vampires – not really part of this world and therefore of no great interest, other than in a fictional sense.'

'What if someone found evidence of them, though?' He threw me a searching look. 'Like, a scale, for instance?'

He saw I was serious and drew himself up to give a sensible answer. 'Well, that would be a strange and unique treasure. But therein lies a major problem.'

'Sir?'

'That word *unique*. How would you prove the authenticity of your "evidence" when there is nothing else to compare it with?'

The bell rang for the end of break.

'Off you go,' he said. 'In the future, I'd advise you to leave crows alone. You don't know what diseases they might be carrying. And try not to bump into any dragons, eh?'

'No, sir. Thanks.' And I dragged myself out of there, none the wiser, but thinking hard about what he'd said.


I was still thinking about it later that night after Josie had gone to bed and Mum and I were in the front room together. I was remembering what Klimt had said about the scale. *We call it dragon because we can find no better word for it.* For him, it didn't matter where the scale had come from. All UNICORNE wanted to know was what it could do, especially when it came into contact with humans. That made me think again about the DVD mystery, prompting me to say to Mum, 'You know the man who fixed the TV aerial, did he go into the attic?'

'Hmm?' she queried.

'The attic, did the TV man go in there?'

'What? Oh . . . yes, I think so. Why?'

'Who was he? What was his name?'

'Sorry?'

'Mum, pay attention! I'm talking to you.'

'I'm recording something,' she said. 'Just a minute.' She was sitting on the edge of the sofa, pointing a remote at the on-screen guide.

I gave an impatient sigh. 'Just find the programme you want and press "OK".' She wasn't the best at this kind of thing.

'I know how to work it, thank you. There's a schedule clash. I'm trying to find an alternative listing. Oh, now look what you've made me do. I've gone back to the silly main menu.'

'Oh, give it to me.' I took the remote from her. 'What's the programme called?'

'*My Lives Remembered*, on channel—'

'I'll find it,' I cut in. Which I did, straight away. She was right; there was a conflict. 'I'll have to change one of your other recordings, because this channel doesn't have repeats.'

'Oh, leave it,' she said, flapping a hand. 'I'm not that bothered. It's just something Harvey ...' She trailed off.

Too late. I'd picked up the scent. 'Harvey?'

She folded her arms. 'The chap from work who's asked me out.'

'His name's *Harvey*?'

'Yes, his name's Harvey.'

'That's a stupid name.'

'Michael! That's horrible. You can go to bed for that.'

'What? It's early.'

'Too bad. That's what being rude gets you. You've never even met this man and already you're against him. Well, I'm not having it. Bed.' She moved her gaze to the door and back. 'Go on. I'm not joking.'

I curled my fingers. I'd played this all wrong. If I was going to find out about the TV man, I needed Mum on my side. Time to use what Josie called drastic tactics. 'Okay, I'm sorry.' I hung my head, made a big show of hugging her, then stood up and turned all sad-eyed towards the door.

'Oh, Michael . . . come back here.'

Yes! Too easy!

She took my hands and swung them gently. 'I don't want us to fight about this. I know how much you love your dad. This is not about replacing him. It's . . . Well, I don't know what it is, to be honest – a TV show. That's what.'

'He wants you to watch something?'

She raised her shoulders. 'Some of the girls at work were talking about hypnosis—'

'Hypnosis?'

'As a possible cure for smoking, and Harvey said there was an interesting thing on tonight about past-life regression.'

'What's that?'

'Oh, a silly idea about people who think they've lived before and remember their old lives under hypnosis.'

Like Dad, perhaps? Was that what was happening to him on the film, when he was talking like a boy?

'Are you okay?' Mum asked. 'You look like you've swallowed an ice cube, whole.'

'Can I watch it?'

'No, it's on late.'

I picked up the remote. 'Okay, I'll record it. Don't get rid of it.' I flicked a few buttons and made sure there was a little red clock next to the programme title.

'You really want to see this?'

'Project – for school.'

'Since when did you study hypnotic regression?'

'It's for . . . biology. Functions of the brain. Who was the TV aerial man?'

'The—? Oh.' That threw her for a second. 'Mr . . . Hart or something.'

'Hart? *Hartland?*'

She looked confused. 'No, that doesn't sound right. I can't remember. I got him from the phone book. Why?'

'Nothing. Forget it. I *am* going to bed now, if that's okay?'

'Fine,' she said. 'Shall I bring you a drink?'

'No, thanks. Mum?'

'Yes?'

'I really am sorry about . . . what I said.'

'I know. Let's put that behind us, okay?'

Yes, but not completely. Hart something? That was worth checking out. And so was this Harvey guy. Much as I disliked the idea of another man in Mum's life, I needed to cover all the angles. Chewing my lip, I said, 'I'd like to meet him.'

'Who, the TV man?'

No. He was one for Freya and her crows. 'Harvey, Mum. I want to meet Harvey.'

**12**
**SNAP**
· · · · · · · · · ·

**I DISOBEYED MUM. ONCE AGAIN, I LISTENED FOR
HER GOING TO BED, GAVE IT HALF AN HOUR,
THEN CREPT INTO THE FRONT ROOM AND**
turned on the TV. I knelt close to the screen and kept the
sound low. *My Lives Remembered* had already started, but I
found the recording and played it from the start, to get an
idea of what it was about. It featured three people, two
men and one woman, who all claimed to have memories
of lives they'd lived before. The first man was a guy called
Hank. He had what Mum would call a walrus moustache
and hair tied back in a skinny plait. Hank lived in Boston,
USA, and drove a school bus. He had never travelled
further north than Montreal, yet he had an irrational fear
of polar bears. He told the story of how a kid had got on

to his bus one morning carrying a stuffed white bear. The sight of the toy had made Hank panic. The fear was so bad he'd had to call the depot to ask them to send a replacement driver. Even photographs of polar bears made him sweat. The next shot showed him in a high-backed chair in a hypnotist's study. He looked exactly like Dad on the DVD, eyes closed, head to one side, words coming out a little slower than normal. The hypnotist asked him who he was. It took a while, but Hank eventually said, *'Tulugaq,'* in a voice that sounded clogged with mud. His Boston accent had completely disappeared. The hypnotist asked him to describe his surroundings. Hank came out with one word, *'ice'*. The hypnotist said, 'Why do you see ice?' After another pause, Hank said, 'Hunting.'

Then it cut to the woman, a nurse who believed she'd met one of her patients during the Crimean War. I skipped that and whizzed the programme forwards, looking for more about Hank. It turned out that in his 'previous life', he'd been an Inuit hunter called Tulugaq (meaning 'raven', weirdly). One day he'd been out hunting for seals when his sled had struck a thin patch of ice and he'd wrecked his knee and been unable to walk. He and most of his dogs were then attacked and killed by a polar bear. He became agitated as he told the story, and needed to be calmed.

'All you hear is my voice,' said the hypnotist. 'I'm going to count from three to one and snap my fingers, then you will wake and be perfectly relaxed. Three ... two ... one ...' *Snap.* Hank cried when he saw the tapes played back. It didn't look to me as if he was faking it.

I sank back and thought about what I'd seen. If this was real and Hank wasn't just dreaming, did that mean we'd *all* lived lives in the past? Me, Mum, Josie, Dad? I turned my thoughts to the DVD, but it was the words of Mr Greenway that kept playing in my head. *How would you prove the authenticity of your evidence when there is nothing else to compare your dragon scale with?* Answer: you'd run a series of experiments on anyone who had come into contact with the scale to record its effect on humans and see if it gave any clues to its origins – or its powers. Was that why Dad had not come home? UNICORNE had held him in quarantine, no doubt calling in Liam Nolan to first run a series of medical checks, before putting Dad through a battery of tests, regression hypnosis being one example. Just like Hank, Dad seemed to be remembering a previous life, in which he was some sort of mountain boy, reliving a time when dragons must have visited the earth. He'd seen them filling up the sky, had felt the air move to the power of their wingbeats, listened to the deafening roar of their cries, marvelled at their breaths of rippling fire. *Galan aug scieth*. I closed my eyes and rocked to the rhythm of those mysterious words. Maybe he'd learnt a snippet of their language. *Galan aug scieth*. But what did it mean? And why would he say it? *Galan aug scieth. Galan aug scieth*. Over and over I repeated the phrase, until I could feel my head turning light. My body swayed. There was heat in my hand, the hand that Klimt had exposed to the scale. My head was a field of expanding stars. I was on the brink of a reality shift unlike anything I'd experienced before. *Galan aug scieth.* My heart raced. I heard a growl and sensed the TV flickering.

'*GALAN AUG SCIETH!*'

My eyes flashed open.

There was a dragon on the TV screen.

And I was ready to go to it, to move through time and be someone *else,* in a different *era*, a different *world*, a different *life*, when a voice cried, 'MICHAEL!' and I became aware of hands on my shoulders, rocking me sideways, shaking me, shaking me, *punching* my arm.

I snapped awake.

And there was Josie in her nightdress, clutching a teddy bear to her chest.

'What are you doing?' she hissed. 'Mum'll kill you if she sees you up this late with the TV on. It's a good thing she doesn't sleep in my room or she'd have heard you and you'd be grounded for EVER.' She hurried forward, grabbed the remote and put the screen to sleep. 'What was that stuff you were saying?'

'I saw a dragon,' I muttered.

'Um, yeah, a trailer for a movie, hello?'

'Trailer?' I panted. 'No, it was real. They were calling me, Jose. I could feel their power.'

'You're *weird*,' she tutted. 'You stay and get caught if you want to. I only came down for Button. At least I've got an excuse if Mum comes in.' She hugged her teddy bear and made for the door.

'Josie, wait.'

'*What?*' She banged a fist through the air.

It was time. This was it. It was time for her to know. I couldn't stand it any longer – the secrets, the lies, the loneliness. Stuff UNICORNE and all it stood for. Stuff the Bulldog and his threats. 'I'm close to learning the truth about Dad.'

Her shoulders sagged. Her eyes closed.

Quickly, I said, 'Think hard. You must remember something about last week? The big office. The soldiers. The paper streamers! A woman called Chantelle changed your memories. She's French. You know her. She was my nurse when you came to visit me in the hospital, after my accident. She was our au pair once . . . in a different reality.'

She looked at me with eyes as small as the teddy's.

'It's true! I'm not lying. Dad worked for a secret organisation. I've got a file on him. I can show you what happened when he went to New Mexico.'

She took a step towards me. 'You're horrible,' she said, her nostrils flaring. 'Don't think I don't know what you're doing.'

I opened my hands. 'What am I doing?'

'You're trying to get me on your side so that Mum will never meet another man. It won't work. And if you make her unhappy by telling her any more of your stupid stories or lies about Dad, I promise I will never speak to you again. NEVER.'

'Jose—?'

But she was gone and I was alone again, questions and theories my only companions.

## 13
### HARVEY

**I MET FREYA ON THE PLAYING FIELDS AT BREAK THE NEXT DAY.**

**'YOU SHOULD BE CAREFUL,' SHE RAKED. 'THE** others will start calling you a loner soon.'

And she, more than anyone, knew what that was like. When she was a girl, she had been the resident outcast at school.

'I don't care what they think. Who needs a dunce like Garvey in their life? I found out about the TV people. It's a company called Hart & Sons. They're on the industrial estate near Holton Woods. I don't know which Hart came to the house. Can't push it with Mum or she'll get suspicious.'

*Ark!* Hart & Sons. That was all she needed.

'Freya, I saw this TV show last night about people who

think they remember lives they've lived before. I'm sure that's what's happening to Dad on the film. Liam was using hypnosis to regress him.'

*Ark?* Why?

I flicked away a blade of grass. 'I don't know. But something strange happened while I was watching.' I told her about the experience I'd had and how Josie had shaken me out of it. 'It wasn't like the reality shifts I've felt before. I've always been at the centre of them, and everything around me has changed the way I imagined it—'

*Ark!* She rustled her feathers.

'Sorry.' She knew all about the shifts, of course. In her case, I'd spun the tracks of the universe and now here she was, strutting around in black feathers by my feet.

She sharpened her beak on a stone.

'This was different, this shift. I didn't feel in control. Maybe that explains why Dad's mind is separated from his body? Maybe they pushed too hard with him when they didn't understand what the scale could do?'

The first bell rang.

I grabbed my bag and stood up. I didn't want to be late again. 'Let me know what you find out about the Harts.'

She gave me that moody look again.

'What?'

*Arrr-aak!* Don't trust UNICORNE.

And away she flew.

The rest of the school day passed without incident. I narrowly escaped yet another detention for turning up in

French without my notebook. Mr Besson, my teacher, let me off with a warning: *Get these verbs copied into your workbook tonight or you'll be writing an essay for me using every one of them.* (I made a mental note to find my workbook.)

It was after school that things took an unexpected turn. While Josie and I were waiting for Mum to collect us, a smart black car oozed into our regular spot. Mum climbed out of the passenger seat.

'Michael. Josie.' She beckoned us to her.

'What's going on?' Josie asked.

I glanced at the driver, a middle-aged man in glasses.

Mum opened a rear door. 'I had to leave my car at work. The battery's dead or something. Harvey offered to help. Come on, it's cold. Get in.'

This was Harvey? I looked at him again, but he was leaning away from me, fiddling with the radio.

*Get in*, Mum mouthed, in that *Be grateful to your grandma for buying you that pair of pink socks you've always wanted* kind of way.

I dropped into the seat. Beige leather. Comfortable. The car was immaculate. It had that just-off-the-production-line smell about it.

'Hello, Michael,' said Harvey. His voice was quiet but confident. A slight American accent.

'Hi,' I grunted, unhappy about being surprised like this. This wasn't the kind of meeting I'd planned for. His eyes appeared in the rear-view mirror, dark brown, no alarming flecks. I found something interesting to look at out of the window.

'Michael, put your seat belt on,' said Mum, helping Josie to fasten hers.

She clunked Josie's door and got into the front passenger seat. The first time that had happened since the weekend before Dad disappeared.

'What kind of car is this?' asked Josie.

'A BMW,' Harvey replied without any hint of smugness.

'It's cool,' Josie said.

It moved liked molten chocolate.

'Do you like cars?' he asked.

'Not really. Michael does.'

Thank you, sister, for that knife in the side.

Mum said, 'He's got a poster of a supercar in his room. Not that you can see it through the plaster dust. A Lamborghini, isn't it?'

I said nothing.

Harvey filled the silence. 'I drove a Lambo once.'

Mum gasped. 'Goodness, you owned a Lamborghini?'

Easily swayed or what?

Harvey laughed. 'Not on a lecturer's wages. I had a drive-day experience at Silverstone racetrack. I took one for a spin around there.'

And broke the track record, no doubt.

'Scared me half to death. They're fast, those things. My foot was more on the brake than the accelerator.'

I felt Mum's gaze on me briefly. 'Well, you won't be going fast around our narrow lanes. Do you need me to tell you the way?'

'GPS has it,' he said.

GPS. That made me think about Dad in the desert, and Mogollon monsters, and encounters with dragons. I happened to glance at Harvey's mirror and saw that he was watching me. I lowered my head and picked at a buckle on my school bag.

Mum reached back and tapped my knee. 'So how was school today, you two?'

Josie piped up. 'Mrs McNiece says I'm ready for my next evaluation.'

'Josie's learning the flute,' Mum explained.

Harvey gave an admiring nod. 'I always struggled with wind instruments. Too many fiddly holes.'

'It's not that hard,' said Josie.

'It is with fingers like mine,' he said. He took a hand off the wheel and wiggled his fingers. He had slightly rough hands, as if he did a lot of gardening or something.

'*Continue forward*,' the GPS said.

'Well, that's excellent, Josie,' Mum said proudly. 'How was your day, Michael? Anything exciting happen?'

Well, I thought about punching Ryan Garvey and had a quick chat with a crow. This was SO fake. Mum never asked about school any more; it was only because her 'friend' was in the car.

'Michael's doing well in religious studies,' said Josie.

'He is?' said Mum.

'Yeah, can't you tell? He's training to be a monk.'

'Get lost!' I snapped, turning on her.

She stuck out her tongue. 'You can still *talk*, then?'

'All right,' Mum said, her voice up a gear. 'Remember where you are, please.' She flashed me a warning glare. 'Moody one, mouthy one,' she said to Harvey. 'I have to live with this daily.'

He smiled, but didn't comment.

'*At the junction, turn right,*' the GPS said.

Harvey turned the corner. 'I can't imagine a life of monastic silence.'

'Certainly not in your profession,' Mum agreed.

'What do you do?' asked Josie.

Like anyone cared.

'I study languages,' he said.

'French?'

He shook his head. 'Bit further east. More ancient Greek.'

Josie wasn't going to miss a chance to show off. '*Je m'appelle* Josie.'

'*Enchanté,* Josie,' he replied.

'What does that mean?' Josie whispered close to Mum's ear.

'I think he said he's pleased to meet you.'

'We can have the GPS in French if you like,' Harvey said.

'Oh, no-oo,' Mum tutted.

'Yes!' squeaked Josie, clapping like a five-year-old.

Harvey tapped the screen a couple of times. The thing immediately said, '*Au croisement, tournez à gauche.*'

Josie rattled with laughter.

Once again, I caught Harvey's gaze in the mirror. Was I

dreaming it or was he trying to read my eyes? Holding my gaze, he said, 'It can be a male or a female voice.'

I looked away, but he'd given me an idea. When Chantelle had been our au pair, she'd taught Josie a lot of French phrases. There was one in particular that Josie liked. *Est-ce que . . . Est-ce que tu . . .* Yeah, got it. I turned to Josie and opened my mouth to speak the whole sentence – only to hear the voice of the GPS say it for me:

'*Est-ce que tu veux un chocolat chaud ce soir?*'

I jumped so high my head hit the roof. The BMW lurched to a halt. We all slammed forwards in our seats.

'Michael?!' Mum gasped. 'What's the matter?'

I stared at the GPS screen, showing us stopped in the middle of the road. 'It said . . .'

'What said?' she snapped.

'Michael, are you hurt?' Harvey asked calmly.

'N–no,' I panted. 'Didn't anyone hear it?'

'Hear *what*?' said Mum. She was furious now. 'Harvey, drive on.'

He put the car into gear and pulled away.

'What . . . what happened?' I said.

Josie made a face. She looked disgusted with me.

Harvey said, 'You were asking Josie if she'd like a hot chocolate, when suddenly you jumped for no reason.'

Me? *I* was speaking? No. It was . . .

Harvey reached out and switched off the GPS. 'Perhaps that spider alarmed you?' He gestured at a light fitting above the rear seats. A tiny spider was rappelling down from it.

I didn't remember seeing *that*.

'Harvey, I'm *so* sorry,' Mum said, which in its fullest translation meant: *He's been like this for weeks; he's driving me crazy*.

Harvey brushed it aside. 'Please, it's fine. No one is hurt and no harm has been done. And look, we're here already.' He pulled into our driveway.

'*What?*' I pressed my face to my rain-spotted window. Mum never got us home as quickly as this. I'd heard about the cow that jumped over the moon, but this felt as if we'd jumped a whole section of road.

Josie got out right away and trudged solemnly indoors.

Mum unclipped her seat belt. 'No one else will say it, but thank you for the lift. You're a gentleman.'

'We'll take care of your car tomorrow,' he said. 'It'll be safe at the college overnight. Actually, Darcy, I'm passing this way in the morning. Would you like me to pick you all up, about eight?'

'Ohhh . . . no . . .' Mum started.

'Really, it's no bother,' he said. 'Josie and Michael will need to get to school, and I believe you have a meeting first thing?'

'Goodness, how did you know that?'

He smiled and said, 'I studied mind reading in Year 10 – or was it simply that you mentioned it as we were leaving the college?'

She laughed and shook her hair. 'Well, if you say so, I must have.'

'Lift?' he prompted.

'All right, if you insist. It would save a lot of messing around with buses, I suppose.'

'Eight it is, then. Bye, Michael.'

I stepped out of the car without speaking.

I looked back to see Mum still apologising for me.

Worse was to come in the house.

'All right, I warned you!' Josie pushed me against the wall.

'Hey! Get off, you little—'

Bang. Not so little these days. And, boy, she was strong when she was wired. 'I said if you upset Mum, I'd never speak to you again!'

'It wasn't me!' I hissed. 'It was the GPS talking! You must have heard it. Chantelle used to ask you if you wanted a hot chocolate before you went to bed.'

That was it. She'd had enough. She slapped me in the chest and 'zipped' her mouth.

Fine. Let her wallow in her ignorance. But something had made that GPS go loopy. And no matter what Mum thought of lovely, charming Harvey, it was all a bit convenient, his passing this way tomorrow.

She came in, dark as a winter sky. 'I realise you're still very young, Michael, but you are *so* immature. Less than twenty-four hours ago, you told me you were keen to meet Harvey. After that dreadful display, it wouldn't surprise me if he moved to another county to avoid us.' And into the front room she went, slamming her car keys on to the tray in the hall.

I looked at those keys for the longest time. And the

more I stared at them, the more I began to wonder. What if I was right and Mum was wrong? What if Harvey was not all he claimed to be? What if the car breaking down had been cleverly arranged so that Harvey could worm his way into our life for some reason? What if he really *could* read minds?

It was time to raise my head above the maze and look around. I was tired of waiting for orders from Klimt. Something was wrong about this whole Harvey business – and I was going to prove it.

Starting with the car.

## 14
### KING

**WHAT MADE ME DO IT, I COULDN'T SAY. I JUST FISHED MUM'S CAR KEYS OFF THE TRAY AND SLIPPED THEM INTO MY POCKET. HOLTON** College was a twenty-minute bike ride from home. All I had to do was find an excuse – and get pedalling.

It didn't take much. I waited till dinner and homework were done. Then I piped up. 'I'm going to Freddie's, okay?'

Mum didn't even blink. 'Home by eight. Not a minute later.' She flapped a hand, dismissing me.

I burned along the country lanes, but I didn't go straight to the college. I stopped at the crossroads between Holton and Poolhaven and tried to figure out what route Harvey's BMW had taken to get us home from school so quickly. I was certain there were only two basic routes, one through town (Mum's normal trip) and the longer run via the coast road. I would have remembered the coast, so we'd definitely come the other way. But how had we got through town so fast? Short of being clamped by an alien spacecraft and taken along at warp speed and dropped, the only explanation I could come up with was a reality shift. I'd been thinking about Chantelle in the car – which might explain the madness with the French GPS – and I'd wanted to be anywhere but in Harvey's presence. So maybe I'd pictured a shorter journey and *bing*, it had simply happened? But if it *was* a shift, it was fuzzy around the edges. Harvey, for instance, had come through unscathed. If I'd wanted to screw up his chances with Mum, I'd have picked out a universe where he was tied up with duct tape in the boot of the car or something. So did that mean I didn't want to mess with an innocent man, or that part of me was trying to accept that it was finally time for someone else to come into Mum's life?

I sighed and got back on to the bike. No. I couldn't let that happen. Dad was here, close, within reach. He could still be rescued. I mustn't ever lose sight of that. I put my head down and pedalled harder. And as I rode towards Holton, I fixed my mind on the one thing that had kept Dad alive for me for years: the chain of paper dragons he'd made. They meant more to me than anything else, those dragons. One day, I would join the chain into a crown, place it on my father's head and say, 'There, you were always my prince, my king. I never forgot you. Welcome home, Da—'

'Oh, good gracious! Look where you're going!'

I braked hard, screwing my front wheel sideways. I'd been so lost in my thoughts I'd almost run over the toes of a woman crossing the road.

'Sorry,' I said, and looked up. Between a couple of spreading chestnut trees was the red-brick frontage of Holton College.

The woman crouched down to pick up a book she'd dropped. She walked away muttering about bikes being 'lethal weapons in the hands of irresponsible children'.

I wasn't listening. I dismounted and pushed my bike along the pavement. I'd seen the college many times before but never actually been inside. It was a beautiful building, three storeys high with a tall, arched doorway and ground-floor windows to match. A stone balustrade ran around the roof. Two men dressed as pirates had once hung a skull and crossbones off it and ranted about cuts in educational spending. According to Mum, that was as lively as her day ever got. She worked in an office at the back of the building, in a student admin role. So that's where I headed, around the main building. In a matter of moments, I was in the car park. Mum's Range Rover was parked close to a wooden fence that separated the college from the neighbouring cemetery. It was one of only half a dozen vehicles present.

I freewheeled over, trying not to appear suspicious. I wasn't exactly sure what I planned to do. I knew nothing about cars, their batteries or engines, but I didn't want anyone getting nosy while I figured something out.

Resting the bike against the fence, I pretended to look at the cemetery for a minute. Two men came out of the college, talking and joking, carrying sports bags and racquets. They paid me no attention, threw their stuff into a car and drove away. As soon as they were gone, I sidled up to the Range Rover, bipped the key fob, got into the driver's seat and closed the door.

Everything looked normal – meaning untidy. Leaves and sweet wrappers on the floor in the back, along with . . . I reached down and pulled my French notebook out from under the passenger seat. So that's where it had gone. Annoying. I opened the glove compartment. A few CDs, the car manual, Mum's driving shades. No listening devices. No wires hanging loose beneath the dashboard. No Harvey-size fingerprints on the gear stick. Nothing to suggest that the car had been tampered with in any way.

I flipped the sun visor down and flipped it back. This was stupid. What was I doing here? What the heck was I expecting to find? I ran my hands around the steering wheel and checked my watch. It was 7.15 already. If I didn't leave soon, I'd be in even deeper trouble with Mum. I reached for the door handle – and hesitated, the car keys jingling in my hand. Should I or shouldn't I try the engine? It was the ultimate test, after all. If the car didn't start, I might as well go home. But if it did . . .

I checked the mirrors. No one around. I made doubly

sure the brake was on – BOY CRASHES INTO CEMETERY was not a headline I wanted Mum to read – then plunged the key into the ignition and turned it. The engine made a fast-clicking noise but didn't fire. I tried it again. Same thing. Flat.

That was it.

Story confirmed.

Done.

I took the key out of the ignition.

And then it happened.

The locks clunked, the headlights started to flash, and the horn went off. *Barp! Barp! Barp! Barp!* Over and over. Loud enough to open every coffin in the cemetery.

'No!' I squealed, and tried the door.

Locked.

I fiddled with the fob, but in my panic dropped it down the side of the seat.

Roomy as the Range Rover was, it adhered to the universal laws of awkwardness where tight spaces were concerned. I fiddled for the keys for what seemed like a week, finally managing to get my fingers on them. I must have pressed a button as I did, because the alarm stopped and the locks clunked again.

Panting like crazy, I pulled the door handle and spilled out on to the tarmac, coming nose to toe with a pair of booted feet. A hand clamped my shoulder. 'Don't even think about running.' And I was hauled up and pinned against the side of the car – by a uniformed security guard.

He was scrawny but mean-eyed, stronger than he looked.

'I'm not stealing it!' I gasped. 'It's my mum's car, honest.'

'Tell that to the judge,' he said.

'Please, I'm not lying!'

'Yeah, and my middle name's Elvis.'

'Actually, Frank, he's *not* lying.'

I looked over the guard's shoulder.

And there was my king for the day.

Harvey.

# 15
## PROMETHEUS

**'YOU KNOW THIS KID, SIR?'**

**'I DO,'** SAID HARVEY. **'I MET HIM FOR THE FIRST TIME THIS AFTERNOON. HE'S MRS** Malone's son. You can put him down now. You wouldn't want a reputation for roughing up minors – and, oddly, you appear to be upsetting that crow.'

We all turned our heads towards the graveyard. A large crow was hunkering on the branch of a tree, looking as though it might attack. I couldn't tell at this distance if it was Freya or one of the others.

The guard reluctantly let me go.

Still with his eyes on the crow, Harvey said, 'Thank you, Frank. I'll take it from here.'

'Strictly speaking, I should log it, sir. Even if he's

known to you, any disturbances should go in the book.'

Harvey smiled. He was thin in the face with lips that moved like loose elastic. He wasn't exactly handsome, but he had that lean, intelligent look Mum liked. He touched his glasses at the bridge of his nose. They were light-weight, practically frameless. A gust of wind could have picked them off with ease. 'I don't want you to log this, Frank.'

The guard blinked. 'But . . . ?'

Harvey's dark brown eyes drilled into him. 'I really don't want you to log this.'

'Well, if you're certain, sir, I'll get on with my rounds.' And Frank drifted away, looking slightly dazed.

The crow, I noticed, relaxed a little.

'Well,' said Harvey, straightening my clothing. 'This is something of a bonus. I wasn't expecting to see you again quite so soon. Might I ask why you're here? Please tell me you *weren't* trying to steal your mother's car?'

'I don't have to tell you anything,' I muttered.

He pushed his hands into the pockets of his trousers, letting his jacket ride on to his hips. He was wearing a straw-coloured polo-necked jumper, almost the same colour as his hair. 'I've just saved you from a serious grounding, Michael. I think that earns me the right to be curious.'

'I came for that,' I said, seeing my notebook on the ground. Thank you, universe. Thank you, Mr Besson.

Harvey leant down and picked it up. 'French,' he said, flicking through it. 'Pity. I was hoping it might be

English.' He smiled and handed the book over.

I gave him a puzzled look.

'Your mother—'

'I've gotta go,' I said, pushing past him. I didn't want to hear him talking about Mum.

'Don't you want to lock the car first?'

Frowning, I paused and bipped the key fob.

The locks clunked and the world seemed to jolt for a second. I heard a buzzing in my ears, and the branches of the trees grew a thin transparent layer before coming back into line again.

Harvey said, 'Oh, by the way, I'd walk the bike home if I were you.'

Walk it? What was he talking about? I yanked it away from the fence.

He nodded at the front wheel. 'You'll do a lot of damage if you ride it like that.'

Oh heck! The tyre was flat.

No way. This couldn't be happening. How could I possibly have a *puncture*? The bike was brand new and riding smoothly. I flashed a look at my watch. It read 7.27. It would take ages to walk home from here. I'd be out with the bins if I was late tonight. Mum was gonna go mental.

'It folds, doesn't it?' Harvey said quietly.

Folds? What folds? Oh, the bike. 'Um, yeah.'

'That's lucky. That means it will fit into the car.' He pointed at the BMW, parked some thirty feet away. I couldn't believe I hadn't seen it on the way in. Some agent I was – snooping right under my suspect's nose!

'You're going to take me home?'

He pulled the keys from his pocket. 'Well, it's either that or I'm planning to steal the bike and sell it on eBay. I know which your mother would prefer. That frantic look at your watch was as bright as a warning flare at sea. What's your cut-off time?'

'Eight.'

He flipped his wrist. His watch had more dials than a space shuttle. 'No problem. We'll easily make that.'

We loaded up the bike. This time I rode in the front, with him.

'I'll drop you out of sight of the house,' he said. 'That way you can walk the bike up the drive and tell your mother you only just got the puncture. Or, if you're smart and the fault's not bad, you can fix it and she need never know. Deal?'

'Deal,' I said, a little stingy with my gratitude. For a guy I hardly knew, he was right on my case. He'd been a boy once, though. I guess he knew the score.

We cruised out of Holton in silence. As we approached the Poolhaven crossroads, it occurred to me to ask about his route yesterday, but the moment I began to speak, he said, 'That crow in the graveyard really did seem taken with you. Do you like crows?'

'Some. They scare me a bit.'

He nodded. 'They are imposing. You should write about it. Writing is a good way of dealing with issues – but I guess you're aware of that.'

Meaning?

He slowed and stopped for a light. 'Your mother told me about your story.'

'*What?*'

He quickly raised his hands. 'She volunteered the information. I have to say, it sounds intriguing.'

I turned away, wanting to SCREAM at my mother. How could she *do* that? How could she share my personal stuff with a virtual stranger?

'And just so we're clear, I know about your father.'

'What?'

The light changed and he eased through the cross-roads. 'His disappearance, I mean.'

Oh. Right. I looked away. Just for a moment, I thought he was about to reveal some vital secret, even show me a tattoo of a rearing black unicorn, a symbol that would tell me he was one of Klimt's crew. I flexed my left ankle, where my personal UNICORNE tattoo was hidden – something else Mum must never know about.

'I think it's brave, what you're doing with your story,' he said. 'Your mother must be very proud of you.'

How much had she told him, I wondered? I picked at my nails and kept my mouth shut. Just because he'd saved my skin tonight didn't mean I had to get chummy with him. This talk about Dad was making me edgy. But Harvey wasn't for stopping.

'I like the idea of the dragon scale. Fascinating creatures, dragons. They pop up all the time in my line of work.'

'I thought you taught languages?'

'That's right, I do. There are quite a few dragons in Greek mythology. You've probably heard of the hydra? Nasty, serpent-like creature. Whack its head off and two more grow back. Charming, eh?'

'Gross.'

He smiled like a man who'd cracked the code to a safe. At last, he had got me talking. 'My favourite legend is the story of Prometheus. It's not about dragons *per se*, but I've always thought there was a link to them. Do you know about Prometheus?'

I shook my head.

'He was a Titan who stole fire from Mount Olympus and gave it to man, angering Zeus – the king of the gods – in the process. I've always thought that "fire", in that sense, had more to do with spiritual empowerment than the flames you'd use to boil a pot of water. In dragon mythology, fire is given to them by their creator. But it's more than just a weapon for frazzling knights; it's a dragon's spark of life, and the source of their powers. Imagine if the Greek texts had been misinterpreted and Prometheus had given men the power of dragons?' He took a hand off the wheel and made a circling movement. 'That would be some combination, wouldn't it?'

'LOOK OUT!' I screamed.

He had turned his head at a vital moment and missed whatever was hurtling towards us. It bounced off the windscreen with a loud *thwap!* Harvey braked. I jumped straight out. Twenty yards behind the car, a black shape lay in the middle of the road.

'No!' I screamed, and went running to it. It was a crow – mangled and bloodied, a wing fluttering like a grounded kite. Its neck was broken, its head turned out. I trembled as I knelt beside it. *Please*, I was praying. *Please, don't let it be . . .*

Just then, another vehicle pulled up beside me. A window slid down.

'Michael?'

I looked up. Dennis.

He unclipped his seat belt and quickly got out. 'What's going on?'

'He hit a crow,' I said.

He looked up and down the road. 'Who did?'

'H—' I began to say his name, but the BMW wasn't there.

Just my bike, lying at the side of the road, and my notebook blowing open in the breeze.

**16**
**CELTIC**

**DENNIS FOUND A RAG IN THE BACK OF HIS VAN AND MOVED THE CROW ON TO THE VERGE. IT WASN'T FREYA; IT WAS ONE OF THE MALES. IT** brought a tear to my eye all the same. Dennis ran a hand along my arm and said, 'It happens, chum. I hit a fox last year, nearly broke my heart. They just run into the road and there's nothing you can do. Birds are even worse, they fly across you so fast.'

'It didn't,' I said.

'Didn't what?'

'Fly across. It came down from above.' As if it was dead before we struck it.

Dennis changed the subject. 'This is your bike, then?' He picked it up off the road. 'You know you've got a flat?'

'What? Oh – yeah.'

'Not your night, is it? Good thing you're almost home.'

I looked along the lane. We were less than thirty yards from our drive. Harvey had done as he'd promised and set me down out of sight of the house. But how had he got the bike out of the car and unfolded it so fast? And why hadn't he hung around to check on the crow?

Dennis wheeled the bike over. 'I'll take a look when I've got the van unloaded.'

'Unloaded?'

'Wood and plasterboard for your ceiling. I was passing this way, so I thought I'd drop off some tools and materials. You can give me a hand, if you want?'

'Will it be heavy?' He was built like Agent Mulrooney, with strong, firm arms. I was like a jellyfish by comparison.

He smiled. 'Not between the two of us. Hopefully, I'll be doing the job later this week.' Another car flashed by. 'Be safe now. See you in a minute.'

He jumped into the van and drove to the house.

Mum's mood improved at seeing him. And when after fifteen minutes of lugging stuff upstairs we went out into the garden to look at my bike, she practically melted with appreciation. He was doing exactly what Dad would have done, not trying to fix the flat but teaching me how to do it myself.

For all that, it confused him a little.

'It's a strange one,' he muttered after we'd both felt around the tyre for a leak. 'It's just literally lost pressure. Yet the valve looks good and the rims are barely tarnished. Got a pump?'

I nodded and went to the garage to fetch it.

Mum perched herself on a low stone bench. I heard her say, 'This is so good of you, Dennis.'

'Any time. Bikes are my passion. Them and my little girl, of course.'

'How old is she?'

'Four.'

'Oh, how lovely. They're gorgeous at that age. Are you planning to have more?'

I saw Dennis shake his head. 'Me and Mel's mother, we're not together any more.'

'Oh, I'm sorry, I didn't mean to—'

'It's all right,' he laughed. 'You weren't to know.'

I stepped back into the garden. 'Here's the pump.'

'I'll go and put the kettle on,' said Mum.

Dennis held up a hand. 'Not for me, thanks. I can't hang around. I'm meeting a friend tonight.'

'Oh, well, maybe next time,' Mum said quietly. Was it me, or was there a hint of disappointment on her face?

He nodded and smiled. 'What are you doing this weekend?'

'The . . . weekend?' That threw her. She touched her fingers to the nape of her neck.

'It's just that Melody will be at her mum's on Saturday, so I thought I might come and fix your ceiling then – save you taking a day off work.'

'Oh, I see,' said Mum. 'For a moment . . .'

For a moment WHAT, Mother? For a moment, you

thought we were all going for a picnic on Begworth Tor? Honestly. Harvey. Dennis. Make up your mind!

'Yes,' she said, flushing slightly. 'That would be helpful. Thank you very much.'

'Right, I'll see you bright and early on Saturday, then.' He jumped up, dusting his hands together.

'What about this?' I held out the pump.

'Attach it to the tyre, blow air in,' he said. He laughed and swept a hand across my hair. 'Give it a go. We'll check it on Saturday.'

The next morning, Harvey turned up at eight, as promised. I was on time for once and Josie was the one holding everyone up – though that probably had something to do with the fact that I'd hidden one of her school socks under the bed so I could get time alone with Harvey.

'How's the bike?' he asked. He was leaning against the car, sifting gravel with the point of one shoe.

'Why did you leave so quickly last night?'

He raised his shoulders, enough to make the arms of his jacket wrinkle. He was wearing the same one as yesterday, with a lighter combination of trousers and sweater. 'You seemed to know the man who stopped. If I'd hung around, he would have known I'd given you a lift and that might have got back to your mother. I was trying to be discreet. Who was that man?'

A devil on my shoulder wanted to say, *A rival for my mother's affections, Harvey*, but all that came out was a tame 'He's fixing my bedroom ceiling.'

'Ah, the great water catastrophe.'

In the background, I heard Mum shouting, 'Oh, get a pair of socks out of the laundry basket for now. We'll sort it out tonight. Come on, Harvey's waiting.'

'Trouble?' he asked.

'No more than usual.'

He smiled thinly. 'By the way, I wanted to ask you something. *Galan aug scieth.*'

For a second, the world moved in slow motion again, not unlike that moment by the graveyard. 'W-what did you say?'

'*Galan aug scieth.* It was scribbled on your notebook. I saw it when I picked it up last night. I meant to ask you about it, but that crow distracted me. It looks like a Celtic language, possibly a variant of Welsh. I was wondering how you came across it.'

'I . . . I saw it in a book.'

'A book about dragons?'

I nodded faintly. 'Do you know what it means?'

'No, but I can make an approximate translation. *Galan* is an ancient word meaning "dragon". But I assume you knew that? This is research for your story, isn't it?'

'Yes,' I said, too breathless to think about deflecting him.

He glanced towards the house. No sign of Mum and Josie. 'Translating words out of context is never wise, but in the roughest sense *galan* means "dragon" and *aug* means "joined to". *Scieth* is the tricky one. The nearest I can get to that is "one I see" or "the one before me". It rather depends who's speaking the phrase. If it was the dragon, for instance, it might use *galan* the way you'd use *boy* to describe yourself as "I". In that example, the word *aug* could also be read as *become*. So if I was attempting a general translation, I would write—'

Annoyingly, Mum came out before he could finish. 'Sorry, Harvey. Silly kerfuffle over socks.'

'I haven't *lost* it,' Josie growled.

'Shut up and get into the car,' Mum warned her. 'You as well, please, Michael.'

Harvey opened the door for me.

I looked into his eyes. They were dancing with crazy flecks of gold. '*I am become you*,' he whispered. 'More literally, *I am you and you are me.* If we assume that *you* is a man, then in the context of your story, the phrase would describe the melding together of your father and a dragon. Powerful imagery, Michael. Imagine the consequences if it were true? Your father, a modern Prometheus. That would make him some kind of god, wouldn't it? You'd better get into the car now. We don't want you to be late for school.'

**17**
**TRIAL**
· · · · · · · · · · ·

## IT STAYED WITH ME ALL DAY LONG, THAT PHRASE. *I AM BECOME YOU.*

I

Am

Become

You.

Was it possible, I asked myself, for humans to not only channel past lives but to recall being something *non-human*?

My grandma used to say, 'Ooh, if I ever came back, I'd be a cat. Warm laps, free meals and no rent. What a life.'

I'd always thought she was loopy.

Now I wasn't so sure.

Something else bugged me all day long. My French

notebook. The words *Galan aug scieth* were scribbled on the back, just as Harvey had said – but weirdly, I couldn't remember doing it. The letters were haphazard and strangely formed, just as if I'd laid my head on my desk, gripped the pen upright and carved the words out in a subconscious daze.

And that wasn't the end of the weirdness.

At lunch, when I went to see Freya, the trees were filled with crows.

'Sit,' she rasped. No warmth this time.

I sat. Warily. 'Is this about last night?'

'What happened?' she caarked.

'I don't know. Harvey was driving normally. The bird just . . . hit.'

*Ark!*

She didn't believe it. Others echoed her call.

I twisted on the stump and looked up into the branches. A host of harsh brown eyes looked back. 'Honestly, it just whacked the windscreen. Harvey had no chance. It fell right out of the sky.'

'No,' she said. 'Raik was watching.'

She gestured at a brute who was often at her wing. He had a strong purple sheen and claws that looked capable of strangling a goat.

*Ark! Aarraak-a-ka!* he said, too fast for me to understand.

'He says Kij was confused, deliberately targeted.'

'Kij?'

'The crow that died.'

'Targeted?'

'Drawn down from the sky.'

'*How?*'

'We don't know. The flock has gathered to hear your words. To find out what you know. To decide.'

'Is this a *trial*?' I glanced at Raik and the crows behind him.

*Arrrk*, he went, quietly puffing his breast.

'Kij was watching over you, Michael. They will blame you for his death unless you can convince them of your innocence.'

And then what? 'You told me once that your crows would never hurt me.'

'No – but we could desert you,' she croaked. 'That might be worse. Tell me exactly what happened last night. Even the smallest thing may be of value.'

'But there's nothing to – no, wait, there is something. Harvey was talking about men having the power of dragons. He moved his hand like this' – I circled mine the way he had – 'and then it happened – the bang.'

I finished the sentence, shaking. If this was going where I thought it was, it would mean that Harvey was what UNICORNE called a Talen – a human with supernatural abilities. That would explain a lot of things – the GPS talking; the hazy jolt of time in the car park; the flat tyre, even. He'd moved his hand in the style of a magician. What if that's what he was, a weaver of spells? And Mum had taken a fancy to him. How long before they started dating? How long before he got into the house?

I jumped up. 'It must have been Harvey. You need to keep tracking him. I need to know where he goes, what he does.'

She tipped her head.

'Freya, you know I wouldn't betray the crows.'

She exchanged a terse *Ark!* with Raik. 'Very well, we believe you. But why would Harvey kill Kij? What does he have to gain by that?'

'I don't know. Maybe it was a warning. He knows you're watching him. He was aware of a crow in the graveyard.'

She turned her head as another bird approached. *Ark!* it cried, causing a confused bustle as it landed. Freya spoke with it a moment, then looked at me again. 'Cil's flock has been tracking Hart and his sons.'

The TV man. I'd forgotten about him. 'And?'

'They have nothing suspicious to report.' She tightened her claws. 'Go carefully, Michael. Raik's flock will be close. We will keep tracking Harvey – and the other man.'

'Dennis? Why would you want to track Dennis? He wouldn't kill Kij. He moved the body off the road.'

'He was there,' she grated. 'That makes him a suspect.'

I shook my head. 'No, not Dennis.'

The school bell rang.

Freya gave a call. The trees emptied of crows.

I hitched up my schoolbag.

Trial over.

For now.

## 18
### ENCOUNTERS

**DENNIS TURNED UP ON SATURDAY MORNING, AS CHIPPER AS EVER. HE WAS WEARING A PAIR OF COMBAT TROUSERS COVERED IN PAINT AND** general work stains. Hanging out of one pocket were a spirit level and a couple of screwdrivers. In another, I could see the flat rectangle of his phone. He looked a sight, but he had that just-got-out-of-the-shower smell about him and his hair was thick and clean. Mum gave him a smile to die for. Cleanliness was high on her list of qualities in the male species. And if you took away the fuzzy beard, even I could see that Dennis was handsome. Josie, who clearly had a bit of a crush on him, said she liked his T-shirt: a picture of a flying saucer with the words I WANT TO BELIEVE printed underneath. He teased her by saying she could have it for ten pounds. She screwed up her nose and politely declined. He smiled and put a cordless drill on the stairs. 'Gonna help?'

'Can't, I've got drama class,' she said.

Dennis laughed. 'I meant your brother.'

I was standing just inside Dad's study, trying to decide what to do, how to play this.

Josie said, 'Hmph, you can shut him in the attic and leave him if you like.'

'Ouch,' said Dennis. 'Sibling wars. Caught in the cross-fire. Not good.'

Mum had overheard all this. She sent Josie away, adding, 'Michael, help with manual labour? You'll be lucky.'

She nearly fainted when I said, 'Yes.' I couldn't bring myself to believe that Dennis had done anything to harm Kij, but I wouldn't find out by avoiding him.

'How's the bike?' he asked as we entered my bedroom. The very same words that Harvey had used. That unnerved me slightly and made me think, *What if they're working together?* I tried not to gulp.

'Tyre's good.'

'Ridden on it yet?'

'No, not yet.'

'But the pressure's stable?'

'Um.'

'Curiouser and curiouser. Give it a spin before I go and we'll check it again. No rush. I'll be here for a while. Grab the other end of this, will you?' He handed me a dust sheet, which we spread out on the floor. He arranged the stepladders in the middle of the room and climbed the first three steps. 'All right, let's get cracking. First thing, find your joists.' He grinned and buzzed his drill. In one quick move, he drilled a hole into the ceiling, locating wood behind the plaster. 'The joists are usually about eighteen inches apart,' he muttered. He moved the drill and made another hole, again hitting wood. 'There. Spot on.' He smiled down. 'You all right? You look like a cat left out in the rain. Still upset about that crow?'

'A bit.'

He nodded and pencil-marked the holes he'd made. 'Pass me the measure, will you?'

I pulled a tape measure off the top of his tool kit. As I handed it to him, his phone made a sound. 'Text?' I said.

He stretched the tape across the shortest width of ceiling. 'No, it's telling me it needs recharging. Meant to do it last night, but forgot.' He skittered down the ladders. 'All right, here's the plan. What we're going to do is create a framework of battens to attach the plasterboard to. Basically a lot of cutting and drilling. You don't have to stay. It's pretty tedious stuff. I'll be fine on my own. I'm the one getting paid for this, remember? Go and ride your bike.'

'It's all right, I'll stay.'

He shrugged. 'As you like.' He picked up a length of wood and measured it.

As he reached behind his ear for a pencil, I said, 'Do you really believe?'

He looked up. 'In what?'

I pointed at his T-shirt.

'Aliens? I want to.' He unwrapped the cable on a circular saw. 'All those billions of planets out there, you've got to believe there's life among them somewhere. Creepy, though, the thought of an alien invasion. I s'pose I'm a bit like you with your dragons; you love the idea of them, but you wouldn't want them terrorising Holton Byford. Think what it would do to the tourist trade.'

I smiled, but the mention of dragons had made me edgy. Was he swinging the conversation on to them deliberately, or was he just being chatty?

Sticking to the ET theme, he said, 'I thought I'd had a close encounter last week, driving along the coast road at night.' He handed me the cable end. 'Can you find somewhere to plug this in?'

I ran the cable to a socket under my desk. 'You saw a flying saucer?'

He crouched down, bracing the wood against his thigh. The blade zinged through it in less than three seconds, leaving a warm smell of sawdust in the air. 'No, it was a bunch of those Chinese lanterns floating out to sea. I had to look twice, though, before I was convinced. You can easily see why people get spooked. I met a man once who swore that aliens had been in his house and rearranged his cutlery.'

'His cutlery? That's stupid.'

He shrugged. 'Aliens have to eat, I guess. I hear the civilised ones like a decent spoon.'

'Yeah, hello. This is Michael you're talking to, not Josie.'

'Hey, don't dis your sister; she's a smart cookie.'

'She's a pain in the bum!'

He hit me with his smile. 'Naturally. It's her job. Don't be fooled by that sharp tongue; she loves you to bits. Here, hold this while I get some screws.' He swung one end of the wood into my hands. He rummaged in a box and took out three long screws, putting two into his mouth and letting the other stand, magnetically, on the end of his drill bit. 'Anyway,' he mumbled, 'better the aliens make off with your cutlery than beam you on to their mother ship. Close encounter of the fourth kind. Scary.' He climbed the ladders, held the wood against the ceiling and drove a screw through it to fix it to a joist. 'There you go. Easy as that.'

'How many kinds of encounter are there?'

'Someone told me seven,' he said, taking the screws from his mouth, 'but I can only remember four. First is a sighting, second is physical evidence, third is contact, fourth requires a note to say you won't be at school the next morning.'

I laughed. He was funny, Dennis.

His phone bleated again. He tutted and dug it out of his pocket. 'I'll switch this off before it drives us both crazy.'

'Is it a Konnia?'

'Yes. You got a charger?'

'Mum has.'

'Do you think she'll mind?'

I shook my head. 'There's a socket on the landing. I can plug it in there.'

'Good lad.' He threw the phone over.

I hurried downstairs and grabbed Mum's charger. I was back on the landing in a matter of seconds, kneeling down checking that the cable would fit, when the phone lit up with a text alert. A thumbnail of the sender appeared alongside it. I let the cable slide away. I stood up, the phone shaking lightly in my hand. Maybe if I'd thought things through a bit longer, I would have played the next few seconds differently. But I went to the bedroom and I said to Dennis, 'You've got a text.'

He blinked. He knew that something was up. 'Yeah? Who from?'

I turned the phone around so he knew I wasn't lying. 'Agent Mulrooney.'

# 19
## TMP
· · · · · · · · · ·

'AGENT?' THAT SEEMED TO CONFUSE HIM.
'WHO ARE YOU – REALLY?' IN LESS THAN TEN
SECONDS, ALL THE WARMTH I'D BEEN BUILDING
up for him had gone. Freya had been right to be suspicious. This could be my crow killer right here.

He lowered his head. 'Michael, I can explain; just give me the phone.'

'It was you, wasn't it?'

'I don't know what you mean.'

'The envelope in the roof. You just pretended it was hidden. You were sent here to plant that DVD. You're one of them. You've seen the film, haven't you?'

'Look, I didn't know what was in the envelope, okay? I don't know anything about a DVD or film. I just . . . Give me the phone.'

He stretched out a hand.

'Fine. You can have it.'

But not before I'd rung Mulrooney first.

'Michael, don't!'

But I was already connected.

'Den?' Mulrooney's voice.

'No. It's me, Michael Malone. I think *Den* wants to talk to you.'

*Then* I passed the phone over.

Dennis snatched it up. A terse conversation followed. 'I don't know. He ... I told you I didn't want any ... Okay, slow down. He's still here.' He held the phone at arm's length. 'He wants to speak to you.'

'Tell him to go and jump off a cliff.'

'He says it's about your father.'

I waited a second, then took the phone from him.

'Tell Klimt I'm tired of his games.'

'This isn't a game, Michael. Anything but.'

'I trusted you, Mulrooney.'

'Michael, listen to me.'

'A few days ago, I saved your life in the Bulldog's office.'

'And I'm trying to save yours now,' he snapped. 'We need to talk, but it can't be on the phone. Meet me at Berry Head. Twenty minutes. The coastal bench where you first saw Klimt.'

'What about Dad?'

'I'll explain when I see you. Twenty minutes.'

He ended the call.

I threw the phone at Dennis.

He caught it against his chest. 'Look, he was calling in a favour, that's all. I know nothing about agents or who he works for or how he's connected to you or your father. I'm just a general maintenance guy.'

'Go. I don't want you in the house.'

He opened his hands. 'I can't *go*. I'm in the middle of a job. What would I say to your mother? I have no more surprises, Michael. When I've finished, you'll never see me again. Period.'

I took a pace into the room. 'Touch Mum or Josie and you're crow bait. Got it?'

'Crows? What have crows got to do with it?'

*Ark!* I screamed.

And there was still enough of the corvid in me to make him lose his balance on the ladders and drain every flush of red from his face.

I left him groaning on the bedroom floor.

*Ark!* Crows.

He got it.


Mulrooney was sitting on the bench when I arrived. It was a calm day, with nothing much happening at sea. Plenty of people were out on the headland, walking alone, or walking their dogs. Help was a shout away if I needed it. I held on to the bike and didn't sit down. Mulrooney leant forward, elbows on his knees, a couple of cigarette butts between his feet.

'I'm sorry,' he said, 'about the play with Dennis.' He stared at the sea, solemn-faced. He had a dark, clean-shaven face, a minor dimple in the middle of his jaw. He was wearing black gloves and a black leather jacket. He looked like an assassin dressed for a hit. 'Sit down. This might take a while.'

'I'll stand, thanks.'

I heard a flutter of wings. Two crows landed ten feet away and started strutting around on the grass. Backup. Good.

Mulrooney paid no attention to the birds. 'I've known Dennis since our time in Special Forces. We ran ops together in the Middle East. One time we were checking an abandoned truck when a device exploded, killing two of our unit. It brought down masonry on a house nearby. Dennis was trapped under rubble. I managed to pull him clear before the smoke dispersed and the snipers sighted him. He's like a brother to me, Michael. He knows nothing about UNICORNE or your dad. There's no way he would have looked at the film.'

'Why did you use him? Why didn't you just show me the film?'

'I couldn't risk exposing myself. I'd been searching for a good way to get the disc to you ever since UNICORNE recruited you. By chance, Den and I were having a drink that lunchtime he came to your house. He told me he was going to look at a roof on one of the old cottages on the outskirts of Holton. When I found out it was yours, everything just fell into place. I asked Den to plant the disc, but to make sure you got it.'

I nodded, remembering how he'd wanted to look inside the roof space, and the sheepish way he'd said, *I, um, just need to get something from my van.* The ceiling caving in had made it easier for him.

Mulrooney went on, 'I knew you'd be smart enough – or confused enough – not to run to Klimt with the disc. I was planning to come clean just as soon as I thought it was safe to do so. You beat me to it, that's all.'

'Safe?'

'That film is red-hot, Michael. If the Bulldog knew you'd seen it, I'd be finished – in any sense you want to imagine.'

'Who shot it?'

'Nolan – secretly, on a cheap spy cam. That's why it's shaky and the quality is bad.'

'How did you get it?'

'He gave it to me.'

'Why?'

'Because he shares my concerns about a boy of your age taking on these crazy missions. He doesn't want you to end up floating in an isolation tank like your father – and neither do I.'

'Klimt told me Liam didn't know about Dad.'

'Maybe not the final outcome, but he knew about the regression experiments. That's his voice on the film.'

I put my bike down. 'What else do you know?'

He ground a cigarette butt into the grass. 'Too much.'

'Did you see Dad when he came home from New Mexico?'

'Briefly, yes.'

'But you came to the house. You were the one who told us he was missing.'

'I was under orders, Michael. And at that time, how could I have known they would drag you into it? Anyway, Thomas wasn't right when he returned. He was feverish, wild, passing in and out of consciousness, talking fast when he did come around. Quantum physics. Computer jargon. Stuff I couldn't begin to understand. Nolan was with him a lot of the time. He said your dad produced page after page of equations, literally wrote on anything he could find. Even Preeve struggled to keep up with the maths. They said that Thomas's mind had been expanded because of his deep exposure to the scale. He was clutching it to his chest when the team picked him up in New Mexico. I heard they had to prise it out of his grasp. They wrapped him up. Put him into what they called elite quarantine. Nolan tried to stabilise him, but conventional treatments didn't work. And bizarre things kept happening. Spontaneous minor reality shifts. Once I saw Thomas walk into a room, disappear out of sight, then walk in again. It was as if he couldn't settle in this world any more. In the end, Preeve sedated him in one of those vapour cubes he used on Freya. It wasn't until they cultured the Mleptra and realised they were a healing influence that the real Thomas began to come back.'

'Then what? Why didn't he come home?'

'He was edgy, keen to work with the scale, not ready to assume domestic cover. Several months had passed by then and we'd put the story into place that he was missing. So we let it run. Hard on your family, I know, but it was his choice as much as anyone's.'

'Yeah, like Klimt had nothing to do with it.'

'Actually, he didn't. Klimt was nothing but a sophisticated toy until your dad came home with the scale.'

'So . . . Dad really did *build* him?'

He sat back, folding his arms. 'I'm unsure of the exact time frame, but the physical prototype was already in place years before your Dad joined UNICORNE. He was involved on the software side and the race to develop a functionally independent android with true artificial intelligence. I don't know all the details. I rarely get to see what goes on in the labs. But if this is Mount Everest,' – he raised a hand above his head – 'then the UNICORNE AI programme is WAY up here.' He raised his hand higher. 'All I know is, they used the scale to accelerate your dad's thinking processes. Whatever they did must have worked, but it proved to be a double-edged sword. From those experiments, they found the breakthrough they needed to develop a level of consciousness in Klimt, enough to allow him to make judgements based on intuitive logic – the same way humans do. Klimt advanced rapidly after that, but at the same time, your dad began to go downhill. Maybe they pushed him too far, I don't know. But that's how valuable he is to them, Michael. He's the man who gave Klimt life. I guess that's why they want to keep him alive – and why they're hoping you can bring him back.'

At last, I sat down. A gull landed nearby, curious to know if we had any food. The crows chased it off in a flash. 'What about the film. Where does that fit in?'

He sighed and punched his gloves together. 'Again, I don't know everything. I get snippets from Preeve, more from Nolan if I twist his arm. There were side effects.'

'To the experiments?'

'Yes. The scale was escalating Thomas's capacity to think, but it kept giving him what he called intense flash-backs.'

'To what?'

'Them – dragons. From the moment he came home, he never stopped talking about the beasts. They came to him at random moments, he said. Gave him insights. Touched what he called his auma, his soul. He began to talk about their lifestyle as if he'd actually *been* a dragon once. He claimed they existed in a parallel universe with wormholes into this one, but it was forbidden by their laws to open them. The fact that they must have been on earth at one time but had left for some reason really bugged him. I mean *really* bugged him. I remember him saying to me, "Why did they abandon us? Why? What happened?"'

'Is that why Liam hypnotised him – to find out?'

He flipped up his collar and looked across the water. 'The constant stream of dragon talk irritated the Bulldog. He wanted his genius IT man back, not some self-obsessed storyteller. He asked Nolan for advice. Nolan came up with the idea of regressing Thomas under hypnosis to see if he could access any part of his mind that could shed light on his obsession, or settle him down. Your dad agreed. The first three days didn't produce much. On the fourth day, they used neural acceleration to boost the process – and what they call The Mexico Phenomenon was born. I showed you the film so you could see what your father went through, what Klimt and the Bulldog want *you* to experience. From what I can gather from Preeve, TMP describes a specific type of real-ity shift, one in which the subject is able to regress through previous lives, deeper than regression hypnosis allows; that merely tickles the surface. You can't see it on the film, but your dad is connected to the scale while Nolan is giving him suggestions. You saw what happened.'

'The fire from his hand? Was that real?'

'No, that was a trick of the light. But there was more that wasn't on the film. You saw Thomas's skin change colour?'

'Yes.'

'It cracked and turned green and scaly, like a lizard's. That's why you see him looking at his arm. His fingernails extended into claws, Nolan said.'

*I am become you.* Men melding with dragons. Just like Harvey had said. I felt sick. 'Who was he shouting at? Who was Pa?'

'I don't know. Nolan told me that, during the previous three sessions, Thomas had taken on the identity of an unnamed boy. Somehow, in that fourth session, it all got out of control and Thomas stopped responding to Nolan's voice. Preeve loaded a syringe with a doping agent, but by then it was too late. Thomas had gone.'

'Gone? Gone *where*?'

Mulrooney turned and looked at me. 'That's what UNICORNE wants you to tell them. Three years ago, my friend, your father, plugged into a deep-seated memory and found a wormhole into a previous life. He visited a world where dragons roamed. The problem is, Michael, he never came back.'

**20**
GIFT
· · · · · · · · · ·

**DAD USED TO SAY THE PROBLEMS THAT FRUS-
TRATED HIM MOST AROUND THE HOUSE WERE
THOSE THAT HAD A SIMPLE SOLUTION BUT**
were hardest to get to. If you had a ladder, for instance,
replacing a tile on the roof was easy. According to Klimt, I
had the means to scour the multiverse and bring my
father home to us. I had the ladder to fix my tile. The
trouble was, did I have the courage to climb it?

I said to Mulrooney, 'What do I do?' I could feel my
eyes beginning to moisten. And for all his toughness, his
Marine Corps training, he wasn't so far from tears
himself.

He said, 'I showed you the film so you'd know what
you were up against. Unless Klimt can guarantee your safe

return, I think you should let your father go.'

The nip of a breeze got under my collar, but it wasn't the wind that was making me shiver. 'I told the Bulldog I'd do anything to get Dad home.'

'That was before you saw the DVD.'

'I can't abandon him,' I said, clenching my fists. 'He's my dad. How can I leave him stranded? You wouldn't have done that with Dennis, would you?'

He turned his head and looked at the crows. They were milling about, bored. Three of them now. 'That was different. I could calculate my odds of survival. You can't say the same about this. You're just a boy, Michael, with another sixty or seventy years in front of you. Don't throw away your future for one uncertain glimpse of the past.'

I turned my face to the big blue sky. A solitary gull was wheeling across it. There were my chances, right there, I thought: a dot in a limitless expanse of nothingness. 'How would I tell them, Klimt and the Bulldog?'

'Refuse. Tell them you've changed your mind. Say you're not prepared to lose your mum and Josie.'

'I can't.'

'You can.'

'No, they'll find a way. Klimt said they've already activated me.'

'Activated you? How?'

'I . . . I don't know. My hand turned green when he showed me the scale. They've done something to me. I know they have.'

I looked over my shoulder to see a brown-and-white

spaniel chasing the crows into flight. The owner called it back, apologising for the fuss. I took the opportunity to scan the headland. In UNICORNE world, spies were everywhere. You could never be quite sure who was watching you. I said to Mulrooney, 'Isn't this risky? Meeting me, alone?'

He didn't even bother looking around. 'I have a general remit to protect you. It wouldn't be difficult to find a reason to be here. What's the agenda with the TMP run? What's Klimt told you?'

'Nothing. I have to sit tight, wait for the call.'

'Strange,' he said, pulling at the cuff of a glove. 'Once they've made up their minds, they don't normally hang back.' He zipped up his jacket. 'All right, I've done what I came here to do. Ultimately, it's up to you, Michael, but I'll be at your back whenever I can. Everything okay at home, school?'

I took a moment.

'What?' he said.

'I don't know. It might be nothing.'

'What?' he pressed.

'There's this man, Harvey. He wants to date Mum.'

He smiled. 'Not really UNICORNE business.'

'What if he was a Talen who could make a crow fly into a car's windscreen?'

That got his attention. 'Go on.'

So I told him about the weird things that had happened, including the non-existent tyre puncture, and how Harvey had always been on the scene.

He stood up and checked the front wheel of the bike. 'You cycled here okay?'

'Yeah, no problem.'

'Then something strange is going down, and I don't just mean your tyres.' He took out his phone and connected to the internet. 'How long has this Harvey guy worked with your mum?'

'I don't know.'

'You've said nothing to Klimt about it?'

'No.'

'What's his surname? Harvey what?' The home page of Holton College came up.

'I don't know. He's in the languages department.'

He thumbed a few pages. 'I've got the staff listings. Delraye. Harvey Delraye. Senior lecturer. That sound right?'

'I guess.'

'Okay, I'll check him out.'

'Should I do anything – try to keep him away?'

He stood up, shaking his head. 'There's an old saying, "Keep your friends close but your enemies closer".' He slipped the phone into his jacket. 'If this man is what you think he is, trying to stop him from seeing your mum will only put him on his guard. Here, take this.' He passed me a card. 'My number's on it. I know Chantelle is your primary contact, but keep this just between us for now. Anything suspicious, text me or call.'

'Okay.' I picked up the bike.

'And, Michael?'

'Yeah?'

'Be kind to Dennis. Trust me, he's one of the good guys.'

When I got home, Mum was in the kitchen. 'Where did you disappear to?' she said. 'I thought you were supposed to be helping Dennis?'

I heard a drill upstairs. 'He's still here?' Despite Mulrooney's parting words, I wasn't really in the mood to see Dennis.

'Yes. He's worked like a Trojan all morning. Phase one almost done, he says.'

'Phase one?'

'He has to come back next week, to plaster over the boards he's put up. Don't scuttle off, I haven't finished.' She closed the kitchen door, blocking my exit to the garden. 'I have something to tell you. You said you wanted to meet Harvey.'

'I already have.'

'Huddled up in the back of his car doesn't count.' She took a breath. 'I've invited him for dinner tomorrow night.'

'Dinner?'

She crossed her arms. 'A short expression meaning "to eat in the evening". It will require the use of cutlery and a reasonable degree of table manners. Napkins might be involved. Don't look at me as if I've invited a serial killer into our home. I am giving you the chance to make amends for that dreadful episode the other night. He told me you were getting along better the other day. You had a nice chat about dragons, he said. I actually think he likes you – strangely.'

'Hi, I'm done.' Dennis tapped lightly on the kitchen door. He saw me and nodded. I nodded back.

'Oh, thank you,' Mum gushed, going straight to him. 'Are you sure you won't stop for a sandwich or something? Another cup of tea?'

'Thanks, but I've got some lunch in the van. I'll let you know when I can get back to skim the ceiling. I'll source one of your roof tiles as well. Should be done by the end of next week. Michael.' He nodded again and Mum saw him out.

'Lovely man,' she said, coming back into the kitchen.

'Sure you don't want to invite *him* as well?'

'Don't start,' she said. 'It's just dinner.'

Yeah, right. How about we bring the pair of them around with duelling pistols? Walk ten paces, guys. Turn. Bang! Bang!

All my problems solved in one go.

My ceiling looked like a flat grey quilt, but Dennis, to be fair, had done a neat job. I was trying to decide how I felt about Dennis, when I saw a white envelope taped to my bedpost. A note had been pencilled on the front. *Don't know if you wanted these, but here they are anyway. D.*

Inside were some fluorescent shapes: stars, crescent moons, a rocket ship, the planet Saturn. Dad had stuck them to the ceiling for me when I was young. They glowed in the dark when the lights were turned off. Dennis had taken the trouble to save them. In a tiny, tiny way, he'd kept Dad alive for me.

I decided then and there I would apologise for ranting at him, when he came back. But how much should I try to explain? Me mouthing off about agents and crows must have made him curious, at least. Hopefully, Mulrooney would smooth it over. And Dennis wasn't the type to blab or ask awkward questions – I hoped.

But Harvey. He was a real unknown. I texted Mulrooney to say he was coming for dinner. He texted back. *Noted. Stay alert, but calm.*

Easy for him to say. Waiting for Harvey to turn up on Sunday was in some ways more nail-biting than the thought of hunting for Dad among dragons. Mum had vacuumed and dusted the front room and laid the best cutlery on the table, along with the napkins and the napkin rings that had been imprisoned in a cupboard for as long as I could remember. 'Wow, a tablecloth,' Josie said, which in three words captured the mood precisely.

Strangely, Harvey was late. Mum had told him seven o'clock. At twenty past, she was hovering by the window, picking at her sweater, weighing her phone.

'He'll come,' said Josie, slipping an arm around Mum's waist. 'What man would let you down? You're gorgeous.'

'I'm just a bit concerned about the weather,' she said.

It was squally outside. If Harvey had been coming by rowing boat, even I'd have been concerned for him.

Suddenly, Josie squeaked, 'There's the car. I'll let him in.'

She scooted to the door.

Mum put away her phone and smoothed her skirt. She looked neat. Unfussy, but pretty. She noticed me watching and said, 'Be nice – please?'

I wrinkled my nose. Neutral. That was the best she could expect. Alert, but calm.

Agent mode.

He came in carrying a shopping bag and a small bunch of flowers. He gave Mum the flowers and pecked her cheek. He touched her arm and called her Darcy. Despite the weather, he was still in his trademark jacket and trousers. Dark polo-necked sweater. Smart tan shoes.

'I'm so sorry I'm late,' he said. 'There was an accident at the Poolhaven crossroads. Quite serious. Police and ambulance. They had to close the road behind me.'

'Accident?' I said, cutting Mum off. At Poolhaven?

'Yes.' He looked me squarely in the eye. 'A dark car followed me through the lights. As it turned away from Holton, it skidded, left the road and hit a tree.'

'Goodness,' Mum gasped.

'I stopped to see if I could offer assistance. That's what held me up.'

'Who was driving?' I said.

'How would Harvey know that?' Mum clucked.

Harvey raised a hand to calm her. 'It was a man, Michael. Youngish, in his thirties. He seemed quite fit. He had . . . a military tattoo on his arm. He was alive when they put him into the ambulance. Hopefully, he'll be okay. Now, please, enough of that. Here, I brought you something.'

He lifted the bag.

'You brought something just for *him*?' said Josie.

'For both of you,' Harvey laughed. 'I confess I *was* thinking of Michael, but in some ways, it might suit you even better. I suspect you'll find some reason to wear it, though I'm led to believe that Michael is the dragon fan of the house.'

'Oh, wow!' gasped Josie as he revealed the gift.

It was a crown.

A crown of dragons.

## 21
### BROTH
· · · · · · · · · ·

IT WAS A SINGLE BAND OF SILVER WITH A RING OF PURPLE DRAGONS AROUND IT, EACH ONE CONNECTED BY A JET OF FLAME TO THE outstretched tail of the dragon in front. Harvey handed it to Josie and she showed it to me. I staggered backwards, needing to hold on to a chair for support. I'd seen it before, the crown. One of the first experiments UNICORNE had put me through was a kind of 'consciousness' trip. They'd strapped me into a transparent pod and immersed me in an amber-coloured, breathable fluid. Somehow, they'd put me into a dream state where I'd seen a black unicorn wearing Dad's paper chain of dragons around its neck. When I'd picked up the chain, it turned into a crown, this crown, the one in Josie's hands.

'Goodness, Harvey, I think you've stunned him,' Mum said.

'I . . . I need the bathroom.' I ran, without looking at any of them. I got to the bathroom and pulled my phone from my pocket, trembling so much I dropped it into the washbasin.

I called Mulrooney.

The call went to voicemail.

I tried again.

Voicemail. Nothing.

On the third attempt, I left a message. 'Harvey's here. And something weird's just happened. Are you okay? He said there was an accident at—'

'Michael?'

*Bang! Bang! Bang!* On the bathroom door. Mum.

'Michael, are you all right?'

I swallowed a little sick and opened the door. 'I needed a pee. What's the problem?'

Her eyes tracked downwards. 'You pee with your phone in your hand, do you?'

'I got a text, that's all.'

She folded her arms.

'It came while I was up here.'

She gave me that disbelieving look that parents and teachers can turn on at will. 'You said you'd be nice.'

'I didn't, *actually*.'

That visibly hurt her. She pushed me deeper into the bathroom. 'Let me tell you something, Michael. Something about Harvey. I could go downstairs this instant and ask him to take back his presents and leave. Is that what you want? Is that what this is about? And do you know something else? He'd understand and accept my request because he's a decent, mature human being. It would make things awkward between us at work, but that will be nothing compared to the rift that will be created at home between you and me and your sister. And you might not feel the pain now, but you will in the months to come, trust me. All I'm asking is that you come back to the table, eat with us, and be reasonably polite. One hour. Do you think you can manage that?'

'How long have you known him?'

'What?'

'How long has he worked at the college?'

She screwed up her face. 'He joined last term, about three months ago. Why?'

'Mum, you don't know anything about him.'

'I know enough to trust my own judgement, I think.' She looked at the phone again. 'Answer your text, then come down, all right? Last chance, Michael. I mean it. Last chance.'

When I got there, Josie was sitting at the dining table. She was wearing the crown and asking Harvey where he'd got it. He was sitting opposite her, looking relaxed. The space next to him had been reserved for me. He flapped a hand and said, 'Oh, I was passing a charity shop and saw it in the window. Cost an absolute fortune.'

Josie laughed and fluttered her lashes. 'A princess only

expects the best.'

'Precisely what I told myself,' Harvey said. 'Let Michael take a look.'

'Not now,' said Mum. She picked the crown off Josie's head and put it aside. 'It's time for our starter.' She put a tureen in the centre of the table.

'Soup?' said Josie, turning up her nose.

'Chicken broth,' said Mum. 'You don't have to have any if you don't want to.'

Harvey opened a napkin and spread it on his lap. 'Well, you can count me in. Chicken broth? Very warming on a night like this. I bet those dragons would go for it.'

'Dragons don't eat chicken *broth*,' scoffed Josie.

Harvey broke a bread roll in half. 'Quite right – a dragon would take the whole chicken. *Raar!*' He made a snatching motion across the table. Josie jumped and giggled like a five-year-old. Even I twitched in my seat. Mum, on the other hand, snorted like a dragon and had to pause with the ladle in her hand.

'Oops,' said Harvey. He threw Josie a wink.

'So what *do* dragons eat?' she asked.

'Do we have to talk about silly dragons?' Mum said.

'Oh, and like school or the weather is better?' moaned Josie.

Harvey backed her up. 'Nothing silly about dragons, Mrs M.'

'Don't encourage her,' Mum laughed, serving him first.

They smiled at each other.

Puke alert.

'I mean it,' said Harvey, who refused to be discouraged. 'They're fascinating creatures. I'm sure Michael would agree?'

Mum raised an encouraging eyebrow and ladled some of the broth into my bowl.

Here, I supposed, was my chance to be 'nice'. 'Um, yeah,' I grunted. I threw in a shrug for good measure.

It was a start.

'If the myths are to be believed,' said Harvey, 'dragons are the most highly evolved creatures in the universe.'

Really? Now he'd got my attention.

Josie wiggled her nose. 'What, more than us?'

'Oh, way more than humans,' he said. 'Not only can they fly and breathe fire, they have no known predators. I wouldn't believe all that nonsense about knights slaying them. It would be a brave man who stood up in front of a dragon, wielding nothing but a sword. Even without fire, their range of powers is extraordinary.'

As he said this, I began to feel deeply uneasy. I'd noticed a sudden shift in his tone. He'd moved away from the idea that dragons were creatures of myth and legend, to the point of view that they were real, as if he'd experienced their 'powers' first-hand. I was about to test his idea on predators with a dragon-versus-nuclear-warhead question, when Josie got in front of me again.

'Yeah, but I bet they can't play the flute.'

Fair point on the 'highly evolved' argument. But Harvey wasn't derailed. 'I think you'll find they could if they chose to.'

Josie speechless was not a sight you saw often. Her jaw dropped so much that the tips of her hair were in danger of dipping into her broth. Annoyingly, Mum prevented that from happening by placing a hand on Josie's shoulder. 'Never mind knights and their swords. I would like to see certain people sitting up straight and wielding their spoon. Harvey, would you like a glass of wine?'

'No, thank you,' he said. 'I'm good with water.'

Mum poured some for everyone.

'So how would they do it?' I asked, finding my voice. 'They'd look stupid, for one thing, holding a flute.'

'And their claws are too big for the holes,' said Josie.

Harvey leant forward to sample the broth. As he moved, the neck of his jumper caught against his jacket and I saw a long red scar behind his ear.

I gasped, almost winded by shock.

He heard me and slowly put down his spoon. Making no fuss, he picked up his napkin and dabbed his lips. Looking at a puzzled Josie, he said, 'Both of you are making the mistake of assuming that the dragon is in its natural form. Their ability to transform their physical shape is their supreme asset, a skill that very few humans are aware of. The dragon would simply take on a form that would give it the dexterity to play the instrument. Now, if you'll excuse me, I need to speak to Michael alone for a moment.' He turned towards me. As he did, everything in my field of vision jolted and blurred, just like that moment in the car park.

And now, when he spoke, it sounded as if his voice was

crossing a vast window of space. He said, 'I've travelled far to meet you, Michael. Considering we share a common bond, you haven't been the easiest Talen to find.'

And he pulled down the neck of his sweater to show me the full extent of his scar, a wound that ran from behind his ear all the way down to the curve of his shoulder. A jagged line made by the slash of a dragon scale. He had indeed come far. All the way from the Chihuahuan Desert. Now I knew exactly who Harvey was. The fourth member of Lynton's research team. The injured archaeologist.

Jacob Hartland.

## 22
### GIANT
• • • • • • • • • •

'MUM, RUN!' I SCREAMED. I THOUGHT ABOUT
GRABBING A KNIFE, BUT INSTEAD PUT MY RIGHT
HAND UNDER MY SOUP BOWL AND TRIED TO
scoop it hard towards Harvey.

My hand just went right through it.

'Michael, please be calm,' he said. 'You of all people
ought to be aware that we're no longer on the same physical plane as your mother and Josie; it merely appears that
we are.'

He gestured at Mum. She was looking at Josie, frozen
in time. She hadn't responded at all to my shout.

'What have you done?' I yelled.

'You know exactly what I've done. I've tilted our reality so we can talk unimpeded, no longer shackled by our

physical bodies. Perhaps a change of scenery will help.'

He swirled his hand as he'd done in the car before the crow had hit. In an instant, the room, the table and the broth disappeared and we were sitting on rocks in the Chihuahuan Desert, right beside the Mogollon cairn. It was night and the air was cool and still, stars spreading across the sky like a spill of sugar grains.

'Better?' he said.

I jumped up, looking around.

'I wouldn't advise an escape attempt. To perform a shift while you're part of this construct could have . . . disastrous consequences. We already have one member of the Malone family lost in the multiverse. Another would seem rather careless, don't you think?'

'Why have you come here?! What do you want?!'

He spread his hands. 'The scale, of course. I assumed that would be obvious. Once you've tasted the power of a dragon, it's very hard not to want more. Who knew how much we humans were capable of, with a little assistance from beyond the stars?'

'You're crazy.'

He reeled back, looking offended. 'Michael, Michael, I'm an academic. We're never "crazy", just obsessively curious. Whatever you've been told about me is false.'

'I don't know anything about you.'

'Please,' he said, shaking his head. 'You may not have recognised me until now, but you do know plenty about me. You're part of the same organisation that got your father out of New Mexico. You've been briefed about his mission there. You certainly know that he escaped with the scale. Strangely, you're not *absolutely* sure what's happened to him, but you know it has to do with reality shifts, the multiverse and dragons. And you know that Rodriguez cut me with the scale and left me for dead. What are you doing?'

All the time he'd been talking, I'd been feeling for a rock I could throw at him. But as at home, nothing here was solid. Everything around me was just an illusion, conjured out of Harvey's mind. Yet, if I concentrated hard enough, I felt I could create some detail of my own. I looked at the stone by my feet and a simple star-shaped petroglyph appeared. I was pretty sure that meant that Harvey didn't have full control of his construct, though the star disappeared the moment I spoke. 'How can you know any of this?'

He tapped his temple. 'It's in your head; that makes it freely available.'

'You've read my mind?'

He pursed his lips. 'Poked around in a few dusty corners when your guard was down would be a better description. A word of warning, Michael: be careful what you bring to the forefront of your mind when a telepath is near. The most immediate thoughts have the strongest echoes. They prick like spikes, demanding to be noticed. *Est-ce que tu veux un chocolat chaud ce soir?* Remember that?'

'You made the GPS say it.'

'No, I made you *think* the GPS said it. It was enough to

shake you up and make you open up to me a fraction more. We need to talk, you and I. There's a lot going on in that lively, jumbled-up mind, isn't there? I'm intrigued about the origin of your powers, for instance. You don't know how you got them, do you? How you went from ordinary boy to a force that could alter the universe. Indeed, most of your "history" is still quite . . . vague. Your peculiar resentment of androids, for instance. And this irresistible fascination you seem to have for crows. I confess I haven't fathomed their significance yet or how you've persuaded them to spy on me, but I applaud your skills of command. Oh, and while we're on the subject of spying, it was silly sending your bodyguard to follow me. It wasn't hard to detect a fellow Talen. Mulrooney, yes? I read his mind when we stopped for petrol. He's fortunate to be alive, Michael. Still, a warning to your masters won't go amiss.'

'They'll kill you if you harm me or my family.'

He smiled broadly, tilting his head the way Klimt often did. 'I doubt it. Why would they want me dead? I'm the most creative subject they've ever encountered.' He blinked his eyes and a small fire ignited among the rocks. He made warming motions with his hands. That gave me an idea of how I might fight him. I looked at the rock in front of me again and tried to imagine a petroglyph of the fire snake Dad had seen attacking Rodriguez. Harvey knew this place well, so the vibrational energy he'd used to make the construct was going to be accurate. If I could tap into it and conjure up a snake . . . ?

'Michael,' he said, snapping his fingers. 'It's polite to pay attention when someone is speaking to you.'

I looked up, fearful that he knew what was in my mind. But his preoccupation with telling me his story had over-ridden his telepathic function. So I let him yak away while I split off a portion of my mind and tried to recall the details of the fire snake from Dad's transcript.

'It's important that you know what happened to me,' Harvey said, 'because it's already happening to you. I read the newspaper article about the dog you rescued on the cliff just recently. You're a talented boy. But you're young, raw, still learning to hone your powers. Three years, Michael. Three years it took my body to adjust once the dragon DNA had fused with my own. It would have been considerably less if those fools at Zone 16 hadn't tried to hinder the changes. After the incident by the cairn, no one could explain the burn marks on Enrico's chest or the radiation levels in his body. So we were put into quar-antine: me, Lynton and Marie. They let Marie and Lynton go soon after, but "quarantine" for me was an ongoing catalogue of stressful experiments. I was caged. Tested. Explored. Probed like a being from outer space. They took pieces out of me, shone lasers into my brain, dosed me with X-rays that almost left me blind, ran so many drugs through my veins that I almost had no circulatory system left. Please, there's really no need to wince; I made sure they paid for it when I broke free. After that, it was simply a question of following the trail of evidence that would lead me to the scale. I tracked down Lynton and discovered he'd been silenced about any link to Stephen Dexter, the bogus archaeologist I'd never met. There was also a trace in Lynton's mind about an interesting man called Thomas Malone, who had apparently gone missing at about the same time Dexter visited New Mexico. After a little research, it soon became clear that Stephen Dexter and Thomas Malone were the same person, and that he was probably working for a covert organisation. So I came to Holton Byford in search of him – and found his son instead. I've lain low since then and bided my time. I've been observing you with great interest, Michael. And look at me now, almost part of the family.'

'You think I'd let you be with Mum, now that I know who you are?'

'Why not?' He sounded scarily serious. 'For one thing, I genuinely like your mother. And who better to nurture you? You and I, we're two of a kind. Quite possibly the only two people on this planet invested with the spiritual auma of dragons. Look at us. Look at where we are: floating beyond the realms of human consciousness. I'm the best father figure you could possibly have. I come to you armed with a range of skills the gods themselves would envy. I can peer into minds, alter my reality, skip through time, engineer constructs like this directly out of my imagination, and very soon, with the scale in my possession, I'll be able to physically transform. I will become a humanoid dragon – a giant among men – and you can be my adopted son.' He stretched a hand as if plucking an apple from a tree. When I looked again, the crown was in it. 'This was one of the most prominent images in your mind. It's a symbol of your father and everything you ever held dear about him. You *want* this, Michael. I know you do. Stay with me and it's yours for all eternity. Trust me, dragons will never leave you. As surely as a vampire craves fresh blood, your need for them will grow at a frightening rate. Unless you satisfy that hunger and learn to control it, it will lead you into darkness.'

'Yeah, and you won't?'

He ran his fingers over the crown. 'You think the people who manipulate you are any better than the scientists who tried to break me? We're on the same side, you and I. We're standing on the threshold of the greatest leap in human evolution since our ancestors emerged from the swamp. Let me teach you something. Around ninety-eight per cent of our DNA is supposedly useless. Your school textbooks will tell you it's junk, redundant material left over from our evolutionary past. They're wrong. Humans are simply a work in progress. These minds, these bodies. We're incomplete. That raw DNA is ready to be coded. All we're waiting for is the right stimulus to take us on to a higher plane of being. You and I have both encountered that stimulus, and look what it's done for us. Doesn't that excite you? The thought of being more than human? Don't kid yourself that your father didn't want it. He knew what it meant to put this on his head.' He held up the crown. 'We need that scale, Michael. Whatever your people have promised you, I can promise more.'

'I don't want your promises,' I growled. And I closed

my eyes and pictured the fire snake as hard as I could. In my mind, I sent it after him, fire spitting from its gaping mouth, hot enough to melt his smug 'academic' face off his head.

I heard a clatter and a scream, but it was me who felt the heat. I jumped in pain and opened my eyes.

And there I was, back at the table at home, with my chicken broth spilled on the tablecloth and hot fluid dripping into my lap.

'Oh, MICHAEL!' Mum was yelling.

And Josie's mouth was even wider than before.

And Harvey was saying calmly, 'Oh, dear . . .'

And there was something alive for a moment in my bowl. It wriggled and fizzled out in front of my eyes. My dying construct.

A tiny snake.

**23**
**GAME**
· · · · · · · · · · ·

**MUM STOOD UP AND CAME AROUND THE TABLE, YANKING MY CHAIR ASKEW SO SHE COULD SEE THE EXTENT OF THE SPILL. 'OH, HOW HAVE YOU** managed that?' There was a pale yellow stain spreading over my jeans, complete with two strands of dried-out chicken, an orange dash of carrot and a splash of something green, maybe a leek. On a better day, it could have won a prize at the school art exhibition.

'I'm so sorry about this,' Mum twittered to Harvey.

'Please don't apologise,' he said. 'It was a complete accident. If I hadn't been filling his head with dragons, it probably wouldn't have happened.'

'It probably would,' muttered Josie, 'knowing him.'

'Stand up,' said Mum. 'Go into the kitchen and take off

those jeans. They'll need to be washed.'

'But . . . ?'

'I'll get you a clean pair. Kitchen. *Go*.'

I stood up glumly and looked at Harvey. He made a sympathetic face, but behind his eyes was an unmistakeable glint of triumph. He'd seen my move and swatted me aside. For now, he was the one who wore the crown.

Mum put me back together and we started again. Somehow, I got through the rest of the meal without any more embarrassing blunders. Harvey chatted amiably throughout, keeping Josie amused with his anecdotes, all the while drawing admiration from Mum. No one seemed to mind how quiet I was.

There was no more talk about dragons.

When we finished eating, I offered to wash the dishes.

Mum covered my hand and squeezed it gently. 'I'll do it later, but thank you for asking.'

Act of forgiveness, or careful assessment of damage limitation?

It was hard to tell.

Harvey stayed for an hour or so. Although I could have gone to Dad's study to mope, I wanted to be with Mum and Josie, just in case Harvey tried anything. He didn't. He was the perfect guest. He showed Josie some tricks with matchsticks. She, in turn, played the flute for him. Together, we all played Cluedo. Bizarrely, I won, though I was pretty sure Harvey swung it my way. Colonel Mustard, in the library, with the lead pipe. In every respect, a better outcome than Michael Malone, in the desert, with the fire snake.

We had coffee, then gathered on the front step to say goodbye: Mum with a carefully considered hug, Josie with a gale-force wave, me with a grunt from the low end of my register.

Harvey backed away, one hand in his pocket, soaking up verbal invitations to return. The wind had dropped and he could afford to amble to the BMW. As he opened the door, he looked back at me, and I knew what I had to do.

'Mum, I want to say sorry to him – properly.'

She blinked in surprise. 'Well, you'd better be quick.'

I ran to the car.

He opened his window, the engine running. 'Michael. How was your broth? Not too hot, I hope?'

I took a deep breath. 'All right, I'll help you get the scale, as long as you promise to help me find Dad – and you stay away from Mum.'

His fingers drummed the steering wheel. 'Harsh bargain. Very well. I agree.'

'What do you want me to do?'

'We need to talk, but not here. Do you like football?'

'Not much.'

'Me neither. In fact, I hate the game. Tell your mother you've accepted an invitation to go and see a match with me on Tuesday evening. I'll make the arrangements to pick you up.'

'But if you don't like football—?'

'We're not going to watch a match, Michael. We're

going to test your powers. Now, shake hands. Let your mother see we've bonded.'

I clamped his hand and immediately felt his power surging into me. 'Look at me,' he said. His eyes were glowing purple at their centres. 'The people you work for do not have your family's best interests at heart. Remember that when they contact you next.'

With that, he let me go and drove away.

'All right?' said Mum as I came back to the house. She crossed her arms, shivering as a night breeze ruffled her top. Josie had already gone inside.

'I said I'd go to a football match with him.'

'Football?' Her hoot could have startled an owl; she knew I wasn't a fan.

I lifted my shoulders and looked away.

'That's quite a big step,' she said. 'I think I should talk to Harvey about that. I'm glad you're making an attempt to be friendly, but I'll be the one who decides when you're ready for that sort of commitment.'

'Mum, I *want* to go, okay?' And I pushed on past her before she could argue.

She didn't understand, but then, why should she? Meeting Harvey had nothing to do with being friendly or watching football – it was all about Agent Mulrooney's advice: I wanted to keep my enemy close.

**24**
**DESTINY**

**MY BIGGEST WORRY WAS, SHOULD I TELL
KLIMT? OR SHOULD I KEEP IT UNDER WRAPS
FOR NOW? I DIDN'T TRUST HARVEY, NOT FOR A**
second, but what he'd said about UNICORNE bothered
me. *The people you work for do not have your family's best
interests at heart.* He could be right. How many times had
UNICORNE misled me? How many times had I found
myself waking up confused in one of their labs or clinics?
They claimed they wanted to bring Dad back, yet one of
their most dependable agents had been concerned
enough to chance his loyalty and warn me of the dangers
of The Mexico Phenomenon. Now he was lying in a
hospital bed. And *still* there was nothing on my phone
from his boss.

I ground some enamel. Paced back and forth. Twanged a rubber band until it broke. After fifteen minutes, I could stand it no more; I caved in and texted Chantelle. I sent a neutral message, hoping she'd say something about Mulrooney. She didn't respond. That made me angry and almost tipped me in favour of siding with Harvey. But just as I was getting ready for bed, the phone did ring – and it was Klimt.

'Hello, Michael.'

I'd almost missed that German accent, though my tetchy response made sure I didn't show it. 'Where have you *been*? I've been texting for a week – and zilch! I thought we were doing this Mexico thing? I've read the file. I'm ready. What's happening?'

He merely said, 'Agent Mulrooney has been involved in an accident. We found messages from you on his phone. You have something to tell me, I think?'

I sank down on the air bed, a hand across my eyes. The voicemails. Drat. I should have realised they'd find them if Mulrooney was hurt. Now I'd have to tell Klimt what I knew. What was the point of holding back? I took a deep breath. 'Hartland is here. Hartland, the archaeologist who was cut with the dragon scale. He's here, in Holton Byford. He works at the college with Mum.'

There was a pause. And then Klimt said, 'I know.'

'What? WHAT?!' I jack-knifed into a sitting position.

'Please, Michael, my aural receptors are really quite delicate.'

'Screw your aural . . . whatevers! What do you mean

you *know* about Harvey?'

'You are still quite loud. I assume it is . . . safe to talk?'

I twisted away from the door. 'Just tell me what you know, you freak.'

'Yet again, you disrespect me, Michael. Remember, the director warned you about that.'

'If the Bulldog had ever told me the truth, maybe I wouldn't be mouthing off now! Why didn't you tell me Hartland was around?'

'If you cast your mind back, you will remember I tried. I was prepared to brief you when I showed you the footage from New Mexico. I told you Hartland had survived his attack. You cut me off, anxious to speak about your father instead.'

'That's no excuse! You could have told me any time.'

'Yes, but in the end, it was safer to keep you unaware, until we knew how Hartland would proceed.'

'Safer? What about Mul—?'

'Indeed, what about Mulrooney? Why did you take him into your confidence?'

I glanced across the room at the stack of albums where I'd hidden the file and the DVD. If I told Klimt the truth about the film, Mulrooney and Nolan were in serious trouble – Dennis, too, if they pressed that connection. Nolan I didn't care about, but I couldn't bring myself to snitch on Mulrooney. 'He came to me on the headland while I was riding my bike. He said it was his job to look after me. He wanted to know if everything was okay. I told him weird things had been happening around

Harvey. He said he'd check it out. I thought he'd go straight to you. Why didn't you *warn* him Harvey was around?'

'Hartland is a powerful telepath. Close contact with an agent carrying knowledge about him could have resulted in bloodshed. Your tip-off demonstrated that.'

'Is he okay? Mulrooney, I mean.'

'He is being cared for in the facility. When he wakes, he will be debriefed.'

When he wakes. That made me feel weak.

'So let us recap the situation. The man who presents himself as Harvey Delraye is, as you say, Jacob Hartland. We were warned by our contacts at Zone 16 that he left their facility some months ago. We suspected he might come looking for Thomas.'

'Yeah, well, he's found my family instead. He was here tonight, having chicken *broth*. Playing board games. Chatting up Mum.'

'That is all?'

'No. When I saw the scar on his neck, he changed his reality and showed me a construct of the Chihuahuan Desert.'

'Good. He has revealed himself sooner than expected. That is what we had hoped.'

'Oh, thanks for nothing! He could have killed me if he'd wanted to.'

'But he did not. And it is most unlikely he will. You are his route into UNICORNE, Michael. What has he asked you to do?'

'Why should I tell you? Why shouldn't I join him and take you down?'

Another pause. It sounded like he was sipping some of the weird blue fluid he seemed to live on. 'Do not forget we are caring for your father.'

'Is that a threat? Are you *threatening* me? You hurt Dad and I'll—'

'What do you think Hartland would do about Thomas if he had the scale? Do you really believe he would take the trouble to search for a mind as powerful as his own, when it would simply be easier to remove your father's life support and forget about him for good? Then there is the problem you pose, of course. Jacob Hartland was merely cut with the scale, in a haphazard act of uncontrolled violence.'

'So?'

He paused again before replying. 'We estimate that the amount of biological material that found its way into his body is up to forty times less than the level in yours.'

'In *mine*? In . . . *my* body?'

'Forty times,' he repeated, but I wasn't listening. I was thinking back to the artefact room and the question he'd never truly answered, and I had never seriously asked.

'You told me my powers had come from the scale, but you never said how. What have you done to me, Klimt? What have you DONE?!'

'A simple implant, nothing more.'

'Implant?'

'A fraction of the scale, just under the skin.'

'You've put that thing INSIDE me? Where?'

'The second knuckle of your left hand.'

I looked at the tiny scar on my finger where a wart had been removed three years ago. They had put a piece of dragon scale there? How? It had been a nothing op. Done in minutes, under a local anaesthetic. Mum had been right there in the clinic, talking to me, holding my other hand while I looked away from the doctor's knife.

'No,' I said, feeling sick.

'You are superior to Hartland in every way,' said Klimt. 'The only reason he seems stronger than you is because he has been aware of the scale for longer. He believes in what it can do. Your persistent scepticism about your powers prevents you from using them at will. Hartland is a dangerous foe, but his drive for supremacy will eventually unbalance him. We have information that suggests his white blood cells have developed antibodies to the few Mleptra that entered his bloodstream. Without the Mleptra, he will struggle to control the dragon element. You, of course, received a careful balance of both.'

'Why?' I said, again not listening. 'Why did you put the scale inside me?'

A second ticked by. 'Your father begged the director to allow it.'

'No! Dad would never put me through this. NEVER!'

'But he did, Michael.'

'Liar! Why would he do that? Why?!'

'Are you certain you wish to know?'

'You bet I do! And you'd better have a really good

story, Klimt, or I *will* join Harvey and together we'll destroy everything you are.'

'Very well. Please try to control your emotions. Shortly after Thomas returned from New Mexico, Dr Nolan gave him some test results.'

'Tests? What tests?'

'Blood tests, Michael, for leukaemia – your leukaemia.'

'What?' My chest felt suddenly tight. *Leukaemia?* I hadn't been expecting that. My illness had ended years ago. Ever since the transplant of bone marrow from Dad, I'd been just fine. Or so I'd thought.

Not according to Klimt. 'The condition was returning,' he said. 'Your chances of survival were estimated to be slim. By then, your father was in quarantine with us and deeply affected by his exposure to the scale. Any further donation of marrow was certain to include the dragon DNA. The implant was your father's idea. He wanted you to have a better chance of life, despite the unknown risks the procedure would impose. The director agreed, on condition you would be ours to maintain and control. Your father gave his blessing. Your destiny was set then and there, Michael. If you survived the implant, you were always going to be a UNICORNE agent and a special Talen – one born out of your father's love.'

## 25
### MEETINGS

**BUT IT DIDN'T FEEL LIKE LOVE. IT FELT LIKE DAD HAD MADE A DEAL WITH THE DEVIL. FOR NO MATTER HOW I PERFORMED AT SCHOOL FROM** now on, or what future ambitions I held, or who I fell in love with, or what family I had, there would always be a UNICORNE mission waiting. I was theirs, to 'maintain and control'. A walking experiment. A mutant.

A freak.

I told Freya this at break the next day.

'Then we are freaks together,' she croaked.

Some small comfort, I guess.

*Ark?!* What has Klimt told you to do?

'He wants me to play it cool and stick to the meeting with Harvey. Keep gathering info. Stay low-key. More orders are coming later, he says.'

'We will watch you,' she rasped, plucking out a feather. I caught it as it spiralled towards the ground.

'No. Harvey will kill you if you try to interfere. No UNICORNE presence, that's what Klimt says. All of the agents are being kept back.'

'My crows belong to no one,' she caarked, setting off a cry among the flock. I thought I heard Raik add, *The skies are ours!*

He was right. You couldn't stop birds going where they wanted to, but that hadn't stopped Harvey from killing one at will. I was about to say, *Okay, but don't make it obvious*, when a boy's voice carried across the playing fields, 'Hey, Malone!'

Ryan Garvey. Again. This time with a gang of friends.

I took no notice and turned back to Freya. But before I could speak, the gang started chanting. *Crow! Crow! Crow! Crow!* adding some screeching *arks!* to pep it up.

'Ignore them,' I said. But the flock was restless. You didn't mock birds like these. Raik dropped down a few branches and landed next to Freya. He let out a brutal call that flew long and low across the playing fields. Ryan and his chums hooted with laughter. *Crow! Crow!* They flapped their arms and kept on coming.

'Don't attack them,' I said urgently to Freya. I knew a crow battle cry when I heard one. Raik was ready to lead a strike.

*Arrrk!* cried Freya, paddling her feet. It angers Raik that you do not *fight*!

'That's what they want. It'll only make things worse.'

*Crow! Crow! Crow! Crow!*

Freya looked me hard in the eye.

Oh, for . . .

Breathing hard, I turned to face Ryan. 'Get lost!' I screamed, stepping towards them.

'Lost!' he mocked, in a lousy imitation of a crow screeching.

*Lost! Lost! Lost! Lost!*

On they came, in arrowhead formation, Ryan leading.

I picked up speed and got close enough to thump my hands into his chest.

Losing next to no impetus, he thumped me back.

Their crow chant changed.

*Fight! Fight! Fight! Fight!*

'Leave me alone!' I pushed him again.

He shoved me off. 'You think you're hard enough, Malone?'

And then we got into the second phase, where the shoving got worse and the stares turned mean and neither one of us was going to back down.

'What's the matter with you?' I snarled. Ryan had always been a first-class jerk. He liked to stretch the boundaries of schoolboy tolerance. We'd had plenty of minor skirmishes before, but he'd never been quite as aggressive as this.

'Crow boy,' he said, and spat on my shirt.

And then I was on him.

We hit the ground together, squirming and kicking as

we tried to trade punches. Physically, we were pretty well matched, but I managed to roll him and sit astride his chest, pinning his arms down with my knees.

'You stupid fool!' I slapped his face, leaving a bright red mark on his cheek.

'Ow! All right, I give in!' he yelped. And the normal (frightened) Ryan came back.

But the normal Michael had taken flight.

'They'll kill you!' I screamed, and slapped him again from the other side.

'Hey, Malone, that's enough,' one of the gang said.

I felt a hand on my shoulder and instinctively whacked back.

'*Awww!*' The boy doubled up with his hands in his groin.

I slapped Ryan again. But in my head, it wasn't him I was hitting. All I could see was Jacob Hartland.

Into the fifth strike, a hand gripped my wrist. 'STOP THAT! STOP THAT THIS INSTANT!'

And I was hauled to my feet by our PE teacher, Mr Dartmoor.

'They started it, sir!'

'Well, I'm finishing it,' he snapped, shaking me around. 'All of you, get to your classes. Now! Not you.' He kept his hand on my wrist. 'Or you, Garvey. Do you need to see the nurse?'

'No,' said Ryan, with a glum sniff. He struggled to his feet, feeling his jaw.

'Dentist?'

'No.'

'Is it right what Malone said? Did you start this?'

Cue the code of schoolboy silence.

'Right,' said Mr Dartmoor. 'Detention. You'll both stay behind after school today. No excuses. Got it?' He dragged me closer. 'If I ever see you hitting anyone again, I'll find you a pair of boxing gloves and you can try three rounds with me, understood?'

'Sir.'

He launched me back towards school.

'You're crazy,' muttered Ryan as I fell into line.

'You're lucky,' I hissed as the branches clattered and the crows hit the sky.

*Ark! Ark! Ark!* came the cries.

I raised a fist to shoulder level, knowing she would see it.

Michael Malone. Still king of the crows.

I couldn't find Josie, so I sent a text at lunchtime. *Got deten. Tell Mum 4 me.*

She texted back. *ur pathetic. njoy bus ride home* (snarly face with tongue out).

Nice. At least she was talking again.

Detention was held in a small room with one locked window. The walls were painted vomit yellow and stuck with random 'crime' posters. If the police ever came to school, this was where they lectured you (or grilled you), I'd been told. I sat down at one of the desks as far away from Ryan as I could get. There were three much older boys in there with us, plus Mr Besson, my language teacher.

'Ah, the usual suspects, I see, plus Mr Garvey and Mr Malone. What an unpleasant bonus. You were fighting, I hear?'

The boy in front of me snorted.

Besson said, 'If you want to clear your sinuses, Richardson, have the decency to use a handkerchief. As for you two heavyweight champs, workbooks out, please. I want an essay from you both on world peace. Two sides, minimum. The rest of you can—'

'Whoa!' went Richardson, cutting him off.

One of the other boys wolf-whistled.

Chantelle had just walked into the room.

'Why, Ms Perdot,' Besson said, grinning like a dog who'd been offered a bone. 'I didn't know you were in the building.'

Neither did I. She had briefly been a supply teacher here – a role set up by UNICORNE, of course.

'Monsieur Besson.' She greeted him with a faint smile.

'Aw, she is *hot*,' I heard Richardson whisper.

She was wearing plain black jeans and a polo-necked top, her dark-brown hair cropped like a strawberry leaf. She said, 'I have been asked to relieve you.'

'Really?' said Besson, unable to claw his gaze from her. She had the most amazing eyes, Chantelle. She could stun another human at twenty paces. Better than that, she could bend them to her will by 'glamouring' them.

'*Oui*,' she said, as if she'd snipped a rose. 'You need to go to . . . the gymnasium and climb a rope.'

I buried a laugh. But Richardson couldn't. 'Whaaat?'

'R-rope?' said Mr Besson.

Chantelle demonstrated a hand-over-hand climbing action.

'I . . . I see,' said Besson, still locked on her gaze. 'G-gym . . . you say?'

'. . . nasium,' she added. 'Now, *s'il vous plaît.*'

'Is he *going*?' Richardson hissed at the others. 'Is he actually going?'

He was. His eyes were completely glazed. Amazing. Love her or loathe her, Chantelle was one stunning – and scary – Talen.

'*Au revoir,*' she said, waving Besson out of the door.

Richardson clapped like a lazy seal.

Chantelle was not impressed. 'Out, all of you. Except Malone.'

'No way,' said Richardson. 'This is the best detention EVER!' He popped a stick of gum and sat back, flipping his foot at her.

'Out,' she repeated, bringing her gaze to bear on him. 'On your hands and knees, now – like . . . a sheep.'

Richardson's mouth fell open slowly. The barely chewed gum tumbled down his shirt.

She didn't even need to strengthen the suggestion. He dropped to the ground and crawled out of the door.

'Sheep,' she called.

'*Baah!*' he called back.

She looked at the others. They jumped to their feet.

Ryan said, 'Can you turn Malone into a monkey, miss?'

'Out,' she said.

He didn't ask twice.

She drew up a chair and sat down to face me. '*Bonsoir*, Michael. *Ça fait longtemps.* I have come to give you your orders.'

## 26
### ADAM
• • • • • • • • • •

**'LOOK AT ME,' SHE SAID. 'DO NOT DEVIATE OR GLANCE AWAY. DO NOT TRY TO READ THE FLECKS IN MY EYES. JUST LOOK AT ME AND** concentrate on what I am saying.'

'It was you, wasn't it?'

'Look at me,' she said.

'You glamoured Ryan to make him fight me and get me into detention, didn't you?'

'Shush,' she said, bringing a finger to her lips. 'I will talk; you will listen. Try not to blink. You may nod or shake your head, but always you will keep your eyes on me. Klimt has told me about your meeting.'

'He still wants it to happen?'

'Yes. You are to make Hartland think you are on his

side, but there are certain things we must blank out, things we do not want Hartland to know.'

'Like wha—?'

'Shush!'

Her eyes were growing bigger and hazier by the second. It was like looking at a couple of chestnuts with a telescope. The more I stared, the fuzzier the world became and the more I stopped resisting. Her voice swept over me like a wave.

'You have no idea how your powers came about.'

'Powers,' I muttered.

'No idea.'

'Nnnoo . . . I . . .'

'You believe you were born with the gift to see flecks because your father was a natural Talen.'

'Dad . . .'

'You believe your father's donation of bone marrow boosted your ability to extraordinary levels. Nod your head if you understand.'

I nodded – at least, I thought I did. Her face was soft-ening and it felt as if my head was stuffed with straw. Her words were coming in broken syllables, like a pane of glass imploding in my brain. I sensed her talking about the scale and felt myself nodding again and again. I became aware of her voice fading – and after a while, I jerked awake, like an old man on a sofa, watching TV.

The room was empty.

I looked behind me. No one around. I checked my watch. It was 3.40. I'd been here roughly twenty-five minutes. Faint sounds of school activity confirmed I wasn't dreaming. I pinched my wrist to make absolutely certain and even had a quick peek *under* the desks, just in case anyone was hiding there. No. I was definitely alone. I remembered being sent to detention and vaguely remembered there were other boys present. And was it my imagination, or had a female teacher come into the room and told us we could leave if we did an animal impression?

Too weird. I grabbed my bag and stuck my head into the corridor. A door opened at one end, and a teacher I didn't know walked through. He glanced at me, glanced into the room and walked on, whistling.

What the heck.

Freedom.

Dennis's van was in the drive when I got home. I found him in the kitchen with Mum and Josie, having yet another mug of tea.

'Here comes the villain of the hour,' Mum said. 'All right, bad boy, let's hear what you've got to say for yourself.'

I dropped my bag. 'I got detention, that's all. It's no biggie.'

'Fighting is not a trifling offence.'

'How did you know I'd been—?'

I glared at Josie.

'Serves you right,' she sneered.

'Maybe I should be going,' said Dennis.

'No, you finish your tea,' said Mum. 'Michael is going to his room, where he and I will continue this discussion later.'

I stabbed a finger at Josie. 'Don't believe *her*. I wasn't *really* fighting.'

'Tell that to Ryan Garvey,' she scoffed.

'You stay out of it, you little—!'

'That's ENOUGH!' Mum was on the front foot now. 'Go to your rooms. The pair of you.'

'Why me? What have *I* done?!' Josie protested.

'I think it's called lighting the blue touch paper,' Mum said.

Josie stamped her foot. She turned to Dennis and said, 'She's horrible. I wouldn't ask her out if I were you.'

'I BEG YOUR PARDON?!' Mum roared.

I looked at Dennis. He was laughing into his mug.

Mum had turned several shades of red. 'Josie Malone, come back here now!'

No chance. Josie had skittered away like a rabbit down a hole.

'I am SO sorry,' Mum said to Dennis.

'Don't be,' he replied. 'Lovely tea.'

Mum's gaze fell hard on me.

'Okay-yy, I'm going.' I slouched towards the front room, stopping for a moment by Dennis's chair. 'Thanks for the stars.'

'No problem. Glad I spotted them.'

He raised a hand and we high-fived gently.

'Stars?' Mum said as I stepped out of the kitchen.

'I scraped some fluorescent shapes off the ceiling.'

'Oh, gosh, I'd forgotten about them.' She lowered her voice, but I was hovering near the door and could hear every word. 'His father put them up when Michael was little. I'm sure he's outgrown them by now, but it was thoughtful of you all the same.'

Through the crack of the door, I saw Dennis stand up. 'Do you think he has? Outgrown them, I mean?' He went to the sink and ran his mug under the tap.

'Oh, I don't know,' Mum sighed. 'He's been so . . . unpredictable lately. Problems at school. Fighting. Suspensions. Arguing with Josie. Arguing with me. Standard teenage fare, I suppose. Annoying, but I can cope with the rage. It's the other things that bother me more. Hey, you don't have to do that.' She took a tea towel off him. 'Leave the mug on the drainer, I'll see to it.'

'Old naval habit. Tidy your berth or do fifty press-ups.'

'I don't think I'm as mean as that,' Mum laughed. 'Navy?'

'Marines. I was decommissioned a few years ago.'

'Goodness, you're full of surprises,' she said. There was a noticeable purr in her voice. I didn't need X-ray vision to be able to sense her admiring his muscles.

'Other things?' Dennis asked, bringing the subject back to me.

Mum moved across the kitchen and opened the freezer. 'It's family. I wouldn't want to bore you with it.'

'No, I'm interested,' Dennis said. 'I was a handful for my parents once. Maybe I can help?'

'I doubt it. Not with this.' A drawer rattled open. 'He's developed some kind of phobia about crows.'

I could sense Dennis narrowing his eyes. 'Why crows?'

'He had a friend who liked them. A girl. She died recently. Very tragic. I don't think he's over it. He was involved in a bad car accident around the same time. Hit-and-run.'

'Ouch. Did they find the driver?'

'No. Michael was in the hospital for a fortnight. I'm worried that he's suffered some psychological trauma. He's been checked by specialists, but they didn't find anything.'

'In London?'

'No. Right here, in Holton. At a private clinic where the old coal mine used to be.'

UNICORNE headquarters. My heart skipped a beat.

It skipped another when Dennis said, 'I didn't know we had specialist medical facilities in Holton.'

'Me neither,' Mum said. 'I have Thomas – my husband – to thank for that. He was ahead of his time with things like health care.'

I saw Dennis tug his ear. 'Michael must miss his dad terribly.'

'We all do.'

'Of course. I'm sorry. I didn't mean to—'

'It's all right. Don't apologise. We're used to it. Michael clings to his father's memory more than any of us. He's writing this incredible story about how Thomas was a secret agent who found a dragon scale in the deserts of

New Mexico.'

Bang. My chest felt suddenly tight, as though someone had slammed a door on my lungs. But it wasn't just because of Mum's revelation; it was the muted way Dennis responded to it. 'Wow. That sounds kind of . . . sinister.' He was thinking about it, turning over in his mind the things I'd let slip about Mulrooney.

Secret agent.

He was wondering if it might be true.

'Coping mechanism,' Mum said, slicing open a bag of frozen chips. 'We all have them.'

I heard movement again, Dennis putting a chair under the table. 'Do you mind if I have a quick word with him? Nothing important. Just a follow-up to something we were talking about on Saturday.'

'Be my guest. Look for an angry swarm of hormones in the study.'

He laughed. 'Shouldn't be hard to find. Thanks for the tea. I'll be back to start the skimming in a couple of days.'

I moved out of the front room, fast. I'd barely made it into Dad's chair when Dennis came in.

'Hey, soldier.'

I lifted my shoulders. 'Hey.'

He looked around the room, staring at the *Tree of Life* picture for a moment. 'Are we cool?'

I shrugged again. 'I guess.'

He moved a pair of socks and sat down on the sofa. 'Nice place.'

'Hmm. It's my dad's study.'

He pointed to the albums where the DVD was hidden. 'His vinyl?'

'Hmm.'

'Do you play them?'

'No.'

'You should. Vinyl. Best sound ever. I collect old records. Mind if I look?'

'Yes,' I said, before he could move. 'Mum . . . doesn't like anything disturbed in here.'

He stared at the stack for a moment, running a knuckle across his lips. 'Fair enough. You spoke to Adam on Saturday.'

'Adam?' The name meant nothing to me.

'Mulrooney. His first name's Adam, not Agent. You heard from him since?'

I shook my head nervously. So he had picked up on the 'agent' thing.

'Only . . . his phone's been dead for twenty-six hours.'

I swallowed hard and was sure Dennis saw it. Where was he going with this?

He looked down at his left hand, bending back the tip of each finger as he spoke. 'I know he was looking after you, Michael. That's what he does: looks after people. Puts his life on the line for others. Listen, whatever you're involved in is none of my business. I just want to know Adam's okay, that's all.'

His eyes came up. But what could I tell him that wouldn't land me in trouble with Klimt?

A never-ending second ticked by.

The hint of a smile touched Dennis's lips. Without another word, he slapped his hands against his thighs as if a bell had rung to end the contest. 'No worries. I expect he's switched the phone off and forgotten.' He stood up and opened the door. 'Your mum tells me you're going to a football match tomorrow?'

So it was on. Harvey must have persuaded her at work. 'Hmm.'

He glanced at *The Tree of Life* and nodded. 'Well, try not to fall asleep. See you Wednesday for a match report, yeah?'

'Wednesday?'

He pointed upwards. 'Ceiling. Plaster. Not finished.'

'Oh. Yeah. Right. See you.'

And out he went.

Dennis Handiman, ex-Marine.

A fly in a now very sticky ointment.

## 27
## BREWERY

**HARVEY ARRIVED ON TIME THE NEXT EVENING, WEARING A BLUE-AND-WHITE SUPPORTER'S SCARF. 'HOLTON ROVERS,' HE SAID. 'THOUGHT** I'd get us in the mood.' He handed a similar scarf to me.

'I'm not wearing that,' I said.

'Yes, you are,' said Mum. 'It'll be freezing in that stadium.'

'Stadium?' Holton was a lower-league team. Their pitch hadn't been upgraded in centuries. It held less than five thousand and its main stand was like a converted chicken coop.

'Doesn't matter. It's open to the cold,' Mum said. 'I don't want you getting a chill.' She proceeded to tie the scarf around my neck. Honestly, it was a wonder I'd ever grown up; she'd be tying my shoelaces for me next. She tucked the loose ends of the scarf into my jacket and zipped it up tight. 'There. Now you look the part. Will he do?'

'Absolutely. Come on you Rovers,' said Harvey.

'Football: it's a mystery to me,' Mum sighed. 'Well, gentlemen, enjoy yourselves.'

Harvey smiled and guided me out of the house. 'Don't worry. We'll have a fantastic time, won't we?'

'If you say so,' I muttered.

He smiled again. 'I'll have him home right after the match.'

The joking ended the moment we were in the car. 'You've spoken to them, haven't you?'

I curled my fingers into a ball.

'Don't waste energy trying to hide it, Michael. I can read them at the front of your mind. Something to do with a black unicorn.'

I immediately thought about the tattoo on my ankle and was terrified to see him glance in the direction of my feet.

'Relax,' he said. 'I expected you to talk to them. Your head's a mess of fuzzy contradictions. Basically, you don't know who to trust. What have they ordered you to do?'

'If you're so smart, why don't you read me?'

He sighed and dropped his shoulders. Even though the temperature was just above freezing, he was still in his academic jacket. As fashion statements went, the football scarf and the leather elbow patches didn't really cut it. He said, 'I'm going to a lot of trouble here, Michael. Please don't disappoint me. Bitterness will only impede our progress. If we're going to be a team, you have to bury your cynicism.'

'Who says we're a team?'

'They do. Your . . . unicorn masters. They want you to shadow me while they work out their plan of *attack*, am I right?'

I tugged my seat belt. 'I don't care about them, or you, or the scale. I just want my dad to come home.'

'And I told you, we'll find him.'

'How?'

He flicked the wipers on to wash the windscreen. Road conditions were damp, but there was no rain in the air. '*Galan aug scieth*. Where did it come from, really?'

I shivered and thought about the DVD. 'Dad. They were doing an experiment with him. The agent you nearly killed gave me a film of it.'

'What kind of experiment?'

'They hypnotised him and asked him to remember a previous life.'

The car swung a corner. 'And?'

'Dad started talking in a really weird voice. He used those words. He sounded like a boy at first and then . . . he was different. His skin sort of changed.'

Harvey was suddenly hungry for more. 'You saw him transform?'

'Just one part of his arm. Then he went a bit crazy and

the film stopped. I don't know what happened after that. The agent you attacked told me Dad's mind had disappeared.' I covered my eyes. It was making me emotional to talk about it.

The car eased over a hump-backed bridge. The Holton Rovers football ground bobbed into view. Harvey tapped the centre of the steering wheel. 'The scientists running the experiment, did they use the scale to boost the effect?'

'I-I think so, yes.'

'Then your father's not lost. His mind isn't wandering the multiverse in search of a home. It's found a new one – with them.'

'With them? With dragons?'

'It's called transference,' he said. He glanced at my startled face and smiled. 'In some of the ancient texts I've read, the most powerful dragons were able to enter another being's mind. They could not only know that being's thoughts, they could commingle with the host's entire consciousness and effectively take control of the body. The dragon could withdraw whenever it wished. But if the process was reversed, if a lesser being, in this case a human, somehow opened a pathway to a dragon, then the human might not be strong enough to return. The dragon mind would simply overwhelm it. The scale could easily be a channel for that. It's my guess that your father's jumped bodies, Michael, and is living among the beasts, alive in their time frame, experiencing their universe.'

'He was a boy,' I repeated.

Harvey nodded. 'That's what makes it doubly interesting. A boy who speaks their tongue and transforms. A human-dragon hybrid. So it *can* be done. Thank you, Thomas Malone. That's perfect.'

Thank you? For what? I had no idea what he was talking about, but at that moment, the car wheeled left and stopped. We were in the car park of Churston Vale, the home of the Holton Rovers Football Club. The main stand and turnstile entrances were in front of us. I understood now why the soccer fans at school gave the stadium the nickname 'the Brewery': on the sign, the *V* was missing from *Vale*.

'Where are all the cars?' I said, looking around. 'Where is everyone?'

Ours was the only car there.

Harvey switched off the engine. 'I told you, we're not here to watch a match. There is no match tonight.'

I panicked then and tried the door. It was locked.

'Michael, what are you doing?'

'Let me out! Why have you brought me here?'

'I told you, to test your powers.'

'How?!'

He unclipped his seat belt. 'What are they planning to do with you?'

'Who?'

'Michael, don't make me angry,' he said. He turned on me sharply, his eyes a blaze of purple. I felt a pinch in my head as his mind touched mine. 'Your controllers. What are they planning to *do*?'

'The experiment,' I said, squirming away from him. 'The same as they did to Dad.'

'The hypnosis?'

'Yes. They call it TMP, The Mexico Phenomenon.'

'Mexico?'

'New Mexico.'

He grunted as if to say, *amateurs*. 'They think they can bring you back from it?'

'I don't know.'

He took off his glasses and polished them quickly. 'Okay. Get out.' He was about to release the locks, when someone tapped on his window and flashed a light inside the car.

Harvey slid the window down.

'Hello. Can I help you, gents?'

It was a man, quite elderly, with puffy sideburns and eyes like boiled sweets. I wasn't sure if he was a security guard or just someone who worked at the club. He sounded more puzzled than threatening.

Harvey said, 'Yes, I believe you can. We'd like to go into the stadium, please.'

The old man switched off his torch. 'I'm sorry, sir, but you've come on the wrong night. There isn't even a training session. The next match isn't until—'

'No, this *is* the right night,' said Harvey. He reached out and grabbed the man's coat, pulling him face to face with him. 'We need to go into the stadium. Now.'

The man's eyes flickered. The sagging skin around them twitched.

'Open the gate,' Harvey said, glamouring him like Chantelle might have done.

'G-gate,' the man jabbered.

Harvey pushed him clear of the car.

The old man staggered towards the main gate, fishing a bundle of keys from his pocket.

'This is crazy; you'll get us into trouble,' I said. 'There'll be cameras and everything. We'll never—'

'Do you want your father back or not?!' he snapped. For the first time, I began to see a trace of Klimt's dark warning, a hint of something inhuman coming through. This was Hartland touched by the monster, the dragon slipping out of control. He said, 'Tonight is the first step in that process. I can do it without you if I have to, Michael. I can break your people, just like I broke them in Zone 16. One way or another, I *will* have the scale. But if I'm forced to retrieve it alone, you and your father become my enemy. We do this together or we fight to the death. Friend or foe, Michael? Which do you *want*?'

'I want Dad back,' I said tamely.

'Good. Then shut up and do as I say. This is where it begins. Get out of the car.'

**28**
VIAL

. . . . . . . . . .

**IT WAS THE EERIEST THING, WALKING ON TO AN EMPTY PITCH WITH NO REACTION FROM THE STANDS. ALTHOUGH IT WAS DARK, THE SKIES** were clear. With the help of the moon, I could see from one end of the pitch to the other, the white lines, the goalposts stripped of their nets, the tunnel between the dugouts that led to the locker rooms, the 'chicken coop' looming like a faceless hoodie.

We made for the centre circle. Harvey was carrying a large leather gym bag that he'd taken off the back seat of the car. One buckle was straining to hold it closed. Whatever was inside the bag had pretty sharp corners. I could see points where the leather was stretched.

In the circle, he stopped and raised his head. 'We've

got company.'

Freya's crows were perched along the roof of the chicken coop.

'This thing with the crows, tell me how it started.'

'There was a girl,' I gulped, wishing more than anything she hadn't followed me. Why didn't Freya ever *listen*? 'People at school used to call her Crow. She died during one of my reality shifts.'

'Died?'

'She changed.'

He put the gym bag on the ground. 'You brought her back – as a bird?'

'It wasn't deliberate.'

He was impressed all the same. 'A secondary change,' he muttered, scanning the crows. 'That's quite a feat. What have your masters *done* to you, Michael?'

'I don't want any birds hurt,' I said. And I shouted at the stand, 'Freya, stay back!'

A couple of quiet *Arks!* pierced the night. None of the birds moved.

'What are we *doing* here?' I clamped my arms. Mum was right. It was freezing tonight.

'Pick a compass point.'

'What?'

He nodded at the four sides of the pitch. 'North, south, east, west.'

'Why?'

'Just do it, Michael.'

I pointed at the steps of the small north terrace, away

behind the goal to my right.

'Good. I want you to go there.'

'But we only just—'

'I don't mean walk there,' he said.

My toes were still inside the centre circle.

'Think back to the day you caught the dog. Did UNICORNE explain to you how you'd moved across the cliffs so quickly?'

'Yeah, kind of.' Klimt had met me on the headland the very next morning. He'd filled my head with a lot of quantum physics, stuff I couldn't really grasp.

'It's called phasing,' said Harvey. 'It's one of the most powerful tools in a dragon's skill set. During the search for your father, you'll need to be able to do it at will.'

I looked at the stand, some fifty yards away. 'I can't; it just happens.'

'You can,' said Harvey. I jumped as he appeared in front of me suddenly. A few crow calls accompanied the move. One crow fluttered across the sky and landed on a flood-light pole. I couldn't be sure, but it looked like Raik.

Harvey said, 'First, you have to let go of the idea that everything around you is entirely physical. What do you know about atoms?'

Really? A science lesson? Now? 'There's . . . a nucleus and electrons spinning around it.'

'And between the nucleus and the electrons?'

I shrugged.

'Space, Michael. Most of the universe is invisible to us. If you removed the space from the atoms of the six billion people on this planet, the human race could be compressed into something no bigger than a sugar cube.'

'So?'

'Dragons knew how to use that space. They knew how to tap into the dark energy of the universe. They used it to move through time. You have that power, but we need to be able to control it if you want to return from this Mexico experiment.'

'We?'

He ignored that and said, 'What was in your mind that morning on the cliff? What were you experiencing just before you rescued the dog?'

'I was frightened. I thought it was going to jump.'

'Frightened. Good.'

'Good?'

'In a heightened emotional state, the human mind is freed from its usual constraints. Suddenly, you can jump higher, run faster, think quicker. You and I can take that one stage further. In our case the impossible becomes attainable; we can alter reality. What was happening here?' He tapped the point between his eyes.

'I . . . imagined myself holding her.'

'Her?'

'The dog. It was a female husky called Trace.'

'And then it happened, the shift?'

'Yes.' One moment I'd been by the car, the next I'd travelled over two hundred yards and was at the cliff edge with Trace squirming in my arms.

Harvey nodded and stepped out of my way. 'Okay.

Look at the stand.'

It was an open terrace with a few crowd barriers, so poorly tended that weeds were growing in the cracks on the steps.

'Picture yourself on it,' he said.

That wasn't hard. I'd been here once before when the lower school football team had made it to the regional final of the Inter-Schools cup. Our headmaster, Mr Solomon, had practically ordered every kid in Year 8 to support them. They lost, 4–0.

I closed my eyes and thought about the match, about standing on that very terrace.

'Now concentrate,' said Harvey. 'Fix your image, then think yourself into the space between the atoms. Imagine your body is nothing but dust, blown from here to there in an instant.'

I tried, but my mind kept drifting. All I could think about was Ryan making up stupid chants and stealing Lauren Shenton's bobble hat, which he'd tried to feed to a passing seagull.

I shook my head. 'I can't do it.'

'You can.'

'I . . . I can't.' I opened my eyes.

I hadn't moved. The terrace, the goalposts, the pitch were all in front of me. My toes were still touching the arc of the centre circle.

Harvey pushed his spectacles higher up his nose. 'Then we need to remove your constraints,' he said.

I heard a commotion among the crows and saw a

dozen of them take to the sky at once. Harvey had opened the gym bag. In his hands was a small, square birdcage.

Inside the cage was a crow.

'Freya?' I gasped. 'Freya? Freya!'

She had keeled to one side, with her legs drawn up and her eyes half-lidded. A band of elastic had been put around her beak to stop her from calling out.

'Don't – move,' Harvey said, placing a deliberate space between the words. 'Step over the line and she dies in an instant.' He meant the line that halved the centre circle. He was in one segment; I was in the other. 'She is "the one", I take it?'

'What have you done to her?' I tightened my fists. Two crows dived at us and spat out a warning. I ducked, but Harvey didn't even flinch. He knew they were far too wary to attack, afraid, like me, he might kill their queen.

'She is . . . remarkable,' he said, staring into the cage. It was a regular pen with thin metal bars, too cramped for a bird of Freya's size. 'I took her yesterday, because they were becoming such a darned nuisance.'

'What have you *done* to her, you freak?!'

'Patience, Michael. I'm getting to that. It was meant to be nothing but a warning at first. It was clear the other birds rallied to this one. So I pulled her from the sky intending to . . . well, throttle her, frankly. But then I had a better idea. I realised you might need a potent stimulus in order to achieve the reality shifts, so I brought her along as a mild incentive. It's only now, of course, that I've discovered just how . . . potent Freya is.' His gaze hardened into mine. 'She's dying. Poisoned. I'd say she has less than two minutes left. The antidote is on the tenth step of one of the four terraces. You can run to the nearest and you might get lucky, but if you really want to save her, you know what you have to do.'

'Which is it?' I begged, frantically looking at all sides of the ground. 'Freya's done nothing to you. Please, Harvey, tell me which one!'

'Dark energy. Space. Phase,' he whispered. He blew a breath across the top of the cage.

I squeezed my eyes shut. North terrace. Tenth step. In my mind, I counted them up from pitch level, pictured number ten as hard as I could. My heart pounded. My breathing quickened. My head felt as light as a bubble. And *bang*! In a flash, I was there. I'd *phased* through time. I'd shifted reality. I hit the steps and immediately lost balance, chafing my shins on the concrete as I slid.

'Careful,' he called, his voice dry with cynicism.

'What am I looking for?' I shouted back.

'A vial, of course.'

I ran along the step. No vial. But on the wall at the end of the terrace, I saw Raik.

*Aaarrk!* What are you looking for?

'Glass. Small. Liquid.' I spoke quietly in crow, because I didn't want Harvey to hear. I tapped the step. 'Ten.' I didn't know if crows could count or if any of what I'd said would make sense to Raik, but he was gone before I could shift again.

I was in the chicken coop stand when I saw Raik next. He was flying across the pitch with something in his claws. The vial. He'd found it! Smart, smart bird. I cupped my hands so he could land and drop his cargo all in one. At the same time, Harvey performed a shift of his own and put himself two steps down, in front of me. He flashed a hand, and Raik went spinning out of control. The chicken coop stand was the only one with seats. Raik hit a seat back and dropped to the floor. The vial clattered away into the darkness.

'What are you doing?!' I cried.

'Cheating is not an option, Michael. Now she dies. Now you'll never find the vial.'

'I can! Please! I just—'

I stopped speaking suddenly – and so did Harvey.

'Move and I'll snap you like a twig,' said a voice.

A strong arm had locked around Harvey's neck.

The arm of an ex-Marine.

Dennis.

## 29
### ZOMBIE

**WHAT HAPPENED NEXT HAPPENED SO FAST I ALMOST LOST ALL SENSE OF TIME.**
**HARVEY DROPPED THE CAGE.**

The floodlights came on.

The crows screeched.

Dennis said, 'Wha—?'

Red dots danced on Harvey's chest.

Voices all around me shouted, 'Armed agents! Stay where you are!'

Dennis cried out as though he'd been punched.

He was catapulted backwards away from Harvey.

My chest heaved with a sudden unexplained breathlessness.

Harvey looked at me with strangely dead eyes.

He veered forwards like a zombie.

The agents shouted, 'STAY WHERE YOU ARE!'

Harvey kept coming.

A flash of light hit him in the chest, dead centre.

Another flash hit him in the head as he fell.

Someone cursed.

People came running.

Then they were on us: six men in black and one woman, Chantelle.

Four of them ran to Harvey. They turned him over. He wasn't moving. One spoke urgently into a headset. Another said, 'No. No. *No!*'

A man I didn't know laid a hand on my shoulder. He spoke with a quiet American accent. 'Michael, my name is Will Reynard. We need to get you out of here. Are you okay?'

I pushed him away and ran to the cage. 'Freya?' I gasped. 'Freya? Freya?' I fumbled with the cage, turning it, looking for any kind of latch. 'HELP HER!' I screamed to anyone who would listen. 'I need to get her out of this cage! She's dying!'

Agent Reynard came to me again. 'Let me,' he said, and put a palm against the bars. Within moments, they'd begun to soften and bend as he somehow applied heat using just his bare hand. He pulled the bars apart and dragged Freya out.

I immediately took her from him and yanked off the band that was binding her beak. It was almost covering her tiny nostrils, but somehow she'd managed to sip enough air to keep herself alive. 'Freya, don't die,' I whispered. My hands were shaking so fast that her head was lolling like an empty glove puppet.

A wild thought flashed through my mind: *You could put her out of her misery now.*

What?

I shook the thought away. As I did, Freya gurgled. Her eyes rolled shut.

'The vial!' I shouted at Reynard. 'She's been poisoned. We have to find the—'

Before I could finish, Freya wriggled, kicked a leg, and thrust out a wing.

'Hhh! Yes! Come on!' I gasped.

And she righted herself and fluttered away. She crashed on to a seat, skittered around on the plastic for a moment, hopped to another seat, skittered again, then took off into the night.

'Freya, wait! We have to—!'

But she was gone, leaving me staring at the sky, wondering about poisons and their antidotes.

'I'm afraid this one's had it,' said Agent Reynard. Raik was laid out across his hands.

I immediately turned and looked for Harvey. If he wasn't dead, I was surely going to kill him. They had laid his body in the aisle between the seats. One of the agents was pressing Harvey's chest in rocking movements.

'Michael!'

Further down the aisle, pitchside, was Dennis. He was on his knees, hands locked together at the back of his head. Chantelle was pointing a laser weapon at him, the same kind they'd used on Harvey.

She said, 'Be quiet. Unless you want to go the same way as him.'

She meant Harvey, of course.

I hurried down the steps.

'Enjoying the game?' said Dennis, through tightly gritted teeth.

Chantelle gave him a warning kick.

'Let him go,' I said. 'He was trying to help me.'

'Stay away, Michael, this is my business.'

'No, let him *go*!' Stupidly, I tried to take the weapon from her, forgetting she was a trained fighter. She grabbed my wrist and twisted me down until I was on my knees beside Dennis.

'Nice friends you've got,' he said.

'All right, Chantelle, enough.'

Reynard came down the steps, gesturing for calm. Chantelle released my wrist. I stayed on my knees, nursing the burn. Reynard sat on the first row of seats, dusting his knees, just like Klimt might have done. This was my first real look at him. He was young, mid-thirties, with a head of black hair too strong to be parted. He had what Mum would call a dreamy expression. There was a kindness in his dark brown eyes that could win a girl over with a single glance. Like Klimt, he was dressed in a suit and tie, but he was altogether more stylish than the android. I didn't know what his connection to UNICORNE was, but I felt I could trust him more than some of the others.

If nothing else, I liked his easy manner.

'Who are you?' he said to Dennis.

'A concerned citizen,' Dennis said tautly.

'He's a builder. He's fixing our roof,' I said.

'A builder with combat training. We don't meet too many of those. What are you doing here – citizen?'

'Making a citizen's arrest,' snapped Dennis. 'How about you? Travelled a long way for a game of football, haven't you? You should have called. I could have told you Holton Rovers aren't worth the price of the ticket.'

'Hands,' said Chantelle, giving Dennis another kick.

Reynard said, 'It's okay, Chantelle, go easy.'

He let Dennis lower his hands to his sides. 'Why did you follow Michael here?'

Dennis squeezed an arm to pump some blood through the muscles. 'He told me he was going to a football match. There are no other stadiums for sixty miles, so he had to be coming to Churston Vale. I knew there was no match here tonight, so I guessed he might be in some kind of trouble. Seems I was right.' He looked sideways at me. 'I want to change my earlier statement: *weird* friends you've got.'

I heard footsteps. 'It's about to get weirder.' Amadeus Klimt was walking towards us. He paused to take a message from one of the agents. I followed Klimt's gaze. Someone had put a sheet over Harvey's body.

Klimt ranged up, dressed, as always, as if he'd been called away from a dinner party. 'Hello, Michael. What unusual surroundings you bring me to. This is not what I meant when I said "low-key". I have just been told that Hartland is dead. Your . . . friend here has caused us many complications.'

'Where's Adam Mulrooney?' Dennis spat.

Chantelle touched the laser weapon to his head.

I got up off my knees and sat down beside Reynard. My head felt strangely buzzy, as if my mind was fast becoming bored with this and wanted to move on. I got myself together and said to Klimt, 'You were the ones who made it complicated; you're the ones pointing the lasers.'

Klimt looked at Reynard for an explanation. Reynard said, 'Hartland appeared to be attacking the boy. I had no choice but to order them to fire. All weapons were set to stun. A beam passed through Hartland's eye as he fell. It appears to be fatal.'

'Careless,' said Klimt. 'Your superiors will not be pleased. I believe that means your work here is done.'

Reynard steepled his fingers. 'There's the small matter of the scale, I think.'

Klimt wafted a hand. 'You came here for Hartland. And now you have him. Our collaboration is at an end.'

'Collaboration? Who are you?' I said.

Reynard tapped his thumbs together. 'I've been tracking Jacob Hartland ever since he escaped from our facility. Mr Klimt has been aiding my investigation, though he hasn't always been as cooperative as my "superiors" would have liked.'

'Your facility? You mean . . . Zone 16?'

He wouldn't confirm that either way. Instead, he said, 'I saved the boy's life, Klimt. That has to be worth something?'

'He helped Freya, too,' I said, thinking back to what he'd done with the cage. Another reason to like him. I glanced at his hands. They looked ordinary enough, but he was clearly a Talen.

'Ah, yes, the troublesome crow,' Klimt said.

'You need to help me trace her. She—'

'Sir, we found this.' One of the men handed Agent Reynard the vial.

'That's the antidote to Freya's poison,' I said.

'Poison?' said Klimt.

Reynard pushed the stopper out of the tube. He ran it cautiously under his nose. 'Nil odour.'

'Please, allow me.' Klimt took the vial and shook the contents. A purple line from his left eye scanned the fluid.

'*What the heck?!*' exclaimed Dennis.

Welcome to the world of artificial intelligence, Dennis.

'It is water,' said Klimt, tipping it away.

'*Water?*'

'Purified. From a bottle.'

I glanced at Harvey's body again. More men had arrived with a stretcher. 'You mean there was no antidote?'

'Quite possibly no poison,' Klimt replied. 'But even if there were, I believe I once took the trouble to explain to you how difficult it is to terminate the undead.'

'*Undead?*' said Dennis.

So it *was* just a test, a trick to make me alter my reality.

All the same, Harvey had made her suffer. If I hadn't flipped that rubber band off in time . . . *She couldn't help you; she was worthless*, a corner of my mind suggested. Uh? That was twice now with the ugly thoughts. Why was I bringing up stuff like that? I shook my head as though to rattle a pea out of my ear.

'You okay, kid?' Reynard tapped my arm.

'Yeah, just . . . an itch.'

The stretcher went past with Harvey on it.

'I don't get this,' I said.

'Get what?' said Klimt.

'Harvey being dead. Why didn't he escape?'

'A laser through the eye is pretty final,' said Reynard.

'But he was cut with the scale; he had dragon powers.'

'*What?*' said Dennis. This was all too much for him.

'And you just shot him like he was . . . normal.'

'Kid has a point.' Reynard looked up at Klimt. 'Maybe I should check it out?'

Klimt twisted the empty vial between his fingers. 'Go with the medics. I will . . . extend our association for now. Continue your investigation with Preeve. Tell him I want a complete and immediate medical report. Mauve priority. Chantelle, you may also leave.'

'What about him?' She gestured at Dennis.

Klimt thought for a moment. 'He is going to help us,' he said. And before anyone could utter another word, he added, 'Someone needs to take Michael home.'

# 30
## MIRROR

**'HOW?' I SPREAD MY HANDS. 'I CAME WITH HARVEY. NO WAY WILL YOU GLAMOUR MUM INTO BELIEVING THAT DENNIS PICKED ME UP.'**

Klimt gestured at Chantelle again. She put away her weapon. She and Agent Reynard left together.

'Stand up,' said Klimt.

Dennis got to his feet.

Klimt said, 'This is what is going to happen. You will drive Michael home and convince his mother that Harvey was called to a sudden emergency. A domestic situation, perhaps. Fortunately, you were in the relatively small crowd, had seen Michael earlier and said hello to him. Harvey approached you during the interval and you offered to help. You, Michael, will tell your mother that

Harvey will be in touch when he can.'

I looked at the disappearing stretcher – and smiled.

'Something amuses you?' said Klimt.

'What? No.' I hadn't meant to smile. What was *wrong* with me? 'Harvey's dead. How are you going to—?'

'Very soon, you will be going in search of your father. Nothing else will matter after that.'

Dennis ran a hand through his thick black hair. 'Will one of you please tell me what is going on?'

Klimt turned to him and said, 'If you wish to be a friend to Michael and his family, you will do exactly as I say. You will forget what you have seen and ask Michael nothing about his work. You will not speak of these events to anyone. If you break this trust, you will never see Adam Mulrooney again.'

'You harm Adam and I'll—'

'Mulrooney is in no danger,' said Klimt, 'but you are. Good night, gentlemen. I trust you will have a safe journey home.'

And with that, he was gone.

'Tell me this isn't happening?' said Dennis. He looked at the night sky and shook his head.

I started walking towards the gate. 'It's your fault. You should have stayed away. Come on, we have to do what he says.'

He grabbed my arm. 'Wait. One question.'

'No. You heard him. You can't ask me anything. He's serious, Dennis. They'll kill you if you get involved.'

'One,' he insisted. 'Is your father alive?'

I nodded silently.

That seemed to trouble him more than the idea of getting killed. He gritted his teeth and stared at the pitch. 'Okay, what the heck. Let's go.'

Amazingly, Mum bought every word. When we got home, Dennis convinced her he was simply being a Good Samaritan. He stayed no more than a couple of minutes, refusing his usual mug of tea.

'Are you okay?' Mum asked him. 'You look a little fraught.'

'I'm fine,' he said. 'Do you mind if I pop into the bathroom before I leave? No need to show me. Think I know where it is by now. Is this Thomas, by the way?' He picked up an old family photograph and studied it.

'Yes,' said Mum.

'Handsome fellow. I see where Michael gets his looks.'

He smiled, closed the front room door and was gone.

Was it me or was he acting just a little bit weird?

It didn't seem to bother Mum too much. She was still wrapped up in her concerns about Harvey. 'Goodness, I feel like a whirlwind's hit us. I hope Harvey's okay. What a peculiar turn of events.'

Huh. Tell me about it.

She sank down on the edge of the sofa. 'I can't quite believe he hasn't been in touch.'

'You never asked him for his number,' I blurted.

'No, I suppose – How did you know we hadn't swapped numbers?'

My brain froze for a moment. Yes. How *did* I know? The sentence had just popped out without my thinking. I shrugged. 'Wild guess, I suppose. It's what people do when they date, isn't it?'

'We aren't *dating*,' she said. 'I like Harvey, but we're a long way from . . . well, we're a long way from anything, really.'

'What about him?' I heard myself saying. The words were stinging, almost envious.

Mum reacted accordingly. 'Him? Who, Dennis?'

*Yes, Dennis*, my thoughts said. 'He left a bit quickly. Maybe he's lost interest in you.'

'I think you'd better go to bed,' she said. 'And be quiet, Josie's asleep.'

*Go*, said my mind. And I turned away with military crispness and left Mum staring into space.

On the landing, I did something I rarely did. I paused at Josie's room, pushed the door wide and looked in. She was snoring as softly as a kitten.

*Shall we wake her?* said my thoughts.

Wake her? I stepped back from the door, holding my head.

What was *wrong* with me?

*Bathroom*, said my thoughts. *Need to go.*

And I headed there and switched on the light. I ran the cold tap and splashed my face.

*Won't help*, said the voice in my head, as if my mind was laughing at me.

I gripped the sides of the basin. What the heck was

going on? I hadn't felt right since the shooting on the terrace. Since . . . I panted and looked up into the mirror.

And there reflected back at me was the face of Jacob Hartland.

# 31
## CONTROL

**I JUMPED BACK AS IF HE'D PUNCHED ME HARD ON THE CHIN, FALLING SO FAR THAT I LANDED INSIDE THE SHOWER CUBICLE. I REACHED OUT** for something to hold and pulled the shower head off its clasp.

Mum was at the bathroom in seconds.

'Michael, are you okay? What on earth's going on?'

I picked myself up from the cubicle floor. 'F–fell . . .' I muttered.

'Fell? How?' She stepped in and replaced the shower head.

'It was him. He's still alive. He's . . .' I covered my eyes. 'He's in my head.'

'Who is? What are you talking about?'

*Tell her,* said the voice.

'Harvey,' I said. And it was *his* voice coming out of *my* mouth. His tone, his American accent.

That spooked her into silence.

'Muu-mm, what's happening?' Josie came along the landing, rubbing sleep from her eyes. 'Oh, it's you,' she said, when she caught sight of me.

I looked straight into her eyes and said, 'Go back to bed. In the morning, you will remember nothing of this.'

Josie froze as if an alien beam had trapped her. Mum gaped at me, then turned to see Josie retracing her steps along the landing. 'Josie?' she said, her voice loaded with confusion. 'Michael, what is—?'

'You need to tell them,' I heard myself saying, but it was Harvey controlling my words, my movements, my glamouring gaze.

'Look, I'm getting tired of this,' Mum said crossly.

Harvey increased the persuasive tone. 'You need to tell them,' he repeated.

'Tell who?'

'The doctor . . . the German.' He was going through my head for information, like a burglar rifling a chest of drawers.

'Dr K,' Mum said, beginning to weaken.

'Yes. Dr K. Dr Klimt.' Harvey raised my hand and made me push a stray curl of hair out of her eyes. 'I'm not well, Mum,' he made me say, letting me revert to my own voice. 'You need to tell them I'm confused, upset about Freya. I need to go back to the clinic. Tomorrow.'

He brought an image of it into my mind, the room they'd put me in, the single bed, the colour of the window blinds, the fishing boat picture that hung on the wall. All there, in an instant, as if he'd opened a cabinet and flipped out a file.

Mum said, 'Yes. I'll . . .' She blinked and stared right through me. Her eyes were so big and green and trusting. Deep inside my head, I was screaming at her not to listen.

But he made me say, 'Call them. You need to call them. Tomorrow. You'll do that, won't you, Mum?'

'Yes,' she said. 'I'll call. Tomorrow.'

'Thanks. I'm going to bed now. 'Night.'

And I kissed her cheek and walked out of the room.

In the study, Harvey started to explain the rules.

'What have you *done*?' I hissed aloud when he gave me back some control of my voice. I immediately tried to scream for Mum, but he locked my mouth in the open position and gagged the muscles of my throat to stop me from breathing. I dropped on to the air bed, fearful he would kill me.

*I can,* he said, *any time I want to. I can terminate you and jump to another host at will. But that would be such a terrible waste when together you and I can achieve so much. When I have the scale, the secrets of the universe will be laid before me. I'm giving you the opportunity to share an unbelievable destiny, Michael, and all you're doing is fighting me. Now, for the last time, do you want to live? I mean really LIVE?*

I nodded as best I could.

He released me slowly. *Then no more attempts to resist. I will be in control from now on. You'll find me a tolerant master – as long as you continue to comply, of course. Please don't imagine you can hide things from me. Your thoughts, intentions and secrets are all mine. I will know, for instance, if you plan to attempt a reality shift. I should warn you, it would be foolish to. Due to the current balance of our 'union', I alone command that power. Try it and you'll be scattered like dust in the cosmos. And how would that serve the quest to find your father?*

'Are you . . . is Hartland . . . dead?' I whispered, working the soreness out of my throat.

*Physically, yes. The body you saw on the ground is a shell. But his – my – consciousness is alive in you.*

'Are we . . . one person?'

I felt him grunt. *You will be Michael when you need to be Michael: a naive boy – with an override function. Think of me as air traffic control.*

'How did you do it? How did you make the jump? You told me it was hard, even for dragons.'

*I have you to thank for it,* he said. Even in thought waves, he managed to sound smug. *Your highly emotional state in the football stadium, coupled with the certainty you needed to generate in order to make the shifts happen by choice, opened a quantum gateway in your mind. All I did was slip through.*

The sudden shock of breathlessness I'd felt.

*Yes, that was me, 'shutting the gate'. You created the perfect conditions for transference. It's almost tempting to believe you sucked me in. In truth, I hadn't planned it like this. I rather liked my old body. Your mother and I would have been a good match.*

'You leave Mum alone. If you make me do anything—'

*Ah-ah, remember who pushes the pain buttons now.*

He made me dig my nails into my palm.

'Ow! All right! Stop it!'

*That was a gentle reminder, Michael. I can cause you a great deal more discomfort than that. Have no qualms about your mother. She would have been a charming distraction, but not enough to divert me from my quest.*

'What are you going to do?'

*Nothing. Sit back. Wait for your android to call. Now that our little deceit is in play, all we have to do is wait for Klimt to take us into the UNICORNE facility, where they'll run their experiment and connect us to the scale. It couldn't be simpler. He's quite an enigma, isn't he, Klimt? A machine given consciousness by your father, though by what means we still don't know. This is exciting, Michael. There's so much to uncover. If I were in your shoes, which technically I am, I would consider it a minor wonder if I slept tonight.*

'What happens, when we sleep?'

He made me emit a chuckle of laughter. He had a laugh like a donkey sucking on helium. I'd hated it every single time I'd heard it.

*This is a round-the-clock service. You sleep, I explore.*

'Explore?'

*All those mysteries swirling in your head. All those question marks about your father. I will sift the facts and make sense of it all. I will be your voice of truth.*

'You're crazy.'

*You need to sleep*, he said angrily, closing my eyes for me, keeping them closed. *One of these days, you'll learn to be grateful that I've given you this chance to experience greatness. Tomorrow, Klimt comes and the journey begins. Tomorrow, you and I become gods.*

## 32
## HEADACHE
· · · · · · · · · ·

**THE NEXT MORNING, I WOKE ON THE AIR BED FULLY DRESSED. CUE ANOTHER TELLING OFF FROM MUM. SHE KNOCKED AND PUT HER HEAD** around the door, just as I was exiting the dozy phase.

'Have you slept in those clothes all night?!'

No, Mum, I decided to change out of my pyjamas at two in the morning, just to annoy you. Why did parents always have to state the obvious?

Harvey took control and I heard myself saying, 'I'm sorry. I couldn't get to sleep for ages. I was . . . frightened. Mum, there were crows at the football pitch last night.'

Clever. He'd sifted my memories and was going to play the Freya card to its max.

It worked. Mum softened a little. She looked me up

and down and said, 'All right. Go and shower. I said I'd call Dr K, and I will. Why are you smirking? Michael, I hope you're not trying to pull—?'

'I need to see Klimt,' I said, in Harvey's powerful glamouring tone. 'Today. No more stalling.'

'Yes, well . . .' She rocked a little. 'I'll . . . I'll see what I can do.'

And out she went.

*Job done*, said Harvey. *Now show me the film.*

'What?'

*I want to see the film of your father's last shift. I found snatches of it in your memory pool. Show me the complete thing. Now.*

I looked across at the stack of albums.

*There's no time to load a DVD*, he said.

'Hey, have they been moved?'

*What?*

'The albums.' They looked different. The spines were uneven.

*I said forget the DVD. The phone. It's on your phone.*

He made me pull my mobile from my pocket.

I ran the clip.

*That's it? Where's the scale?*

'I don't know.'

*How was Thomas connected to it?*

'I don't know. Agh!' I felt a sudden, painful jabbing in my head.

*I told you, don't play games with me, Michael. Last night I searched for the root of your powers and discovered what*

*UNICORNE has done to you. You're carrying dragon implants. One inside your knuckle joint, the other under the tattoo on your ankle.*

Two implants? 'Agh!' He jabbed me again.

*You've also experienced the power of transformation and the thrill of flight. You didn't think to TELL me this?*

'Harvey, stop it! Please.' I rolled on to my side as the pain in my head burned deeper. 'I haven't lied! You told me I couldn't hide anything from you!'

*Then they've interfered. Tried to block out certain memories. But they left in the transformational incident. Interesting. Well, I envy you, Michael. At least now I understand your devotion to Freya. You're more than a boy and his microdots of dragon scale; you have a hint of crow in you, too.*

'No, UNICORNE got rid of the crow.'

*Wrong. They suppressed it, but it's still there. I could chase it down, but it might be of use to us. So my question remains: how was Thomas connected to the scale? If they used it in you, they must have tried something similar with him.*

'Hey, sleepyhead. I thought you were showering?' Mum knocked on the door and went on her way, barking orders to Josie.

*She's right. We can muse on the way to the facility. Get showered.*

'With you looking through my eyes? No way.'

Again, he ramped up the pain. *I told you, you'll be Michael when I need you to be Michael. You don't want to stink for Dr Klimt, do you?*

And he fired the necessary leg responses that launched

me into the hall. I almost knocked Josie off her feet in the process.

'Hey, watch where you're going!'

*Ignore her.* Harvey jerked me away.

'You try ignoring her,' I said out loud.

'What?' said Josie.

He let me look back.

'No more glamouring,' I hissed. 'Leave her alone.'

'What?' she said again, screwing up her nose.

'Jose, just . . . go.'

'You're weird,' she muttered. She shouldered her way through the front room door. 'Mum, Michael's talking to himself. I think he's got an imaginary friend. Probably 'cause no one else will have him.'

'Shush, I'm on the phone,' I heard Mum reply.

I made my way up the stairs. 'You need to be careful with Josie. She's not stupid.'

*By the end of the day, none of this will matter. All human life will be ours to command.*

'I'm not – agh!'

This time, he went too far with the pain and I lost my footing and fell three steps.

Mum and Josie were immediately in the hall.

Mum pounded up the stairs and gripped my shoulders. 'Michael? Are you okay? What happened?'

'My head . . .'

'Mum, what's *wrong* with him?' No sibling angst in Josie now. She was just a genuinely concerned little sister.

'Come on, downstairs, into the front room,' said Mum.

She guided me there and sat me on the sofa.

She took off my shoes. 'Lie down, rest. You're not going to school today. I just spoke to Dr K. He's sending a car for you. Once and for all, we're going to figure this out.'

*Ah, well, forget the shower,* said Harvey. *What's a little body odour between friends?*

The doorbell rang.

'Oh, who's that now?' Mum tutted. 'It can't be your car already.'

'I'll get it,' said Josie. She backed out into the hall.

'You look pale,' Mum said. She smoothed my forehead.

'Please don't,' I whispered. I couldn't bear the thought of her comforting Harvey.

'Sorry, signed up for this thirteen years ago. Loving you is all part of the job.' She rested her hand on my cheek.

From the hallway, Josie shouted, 'Mum, it's Dennis.'

She sighed and said quietly, 'Oh, Dennis, not now.'

But he was in the room already. Jeans and sweater, not his usual work clothes. He had a tablet computer in his hands. He glanced anxiously at me. 'Problem?'

'Bad headache,' Mum said. 'The doctor's on his way. We weren't expecting you this morning, were we?'

'No.' He seemed hesitant. Fired up. Nervous. 'Can I have a word with you, Darcy – in private?' He gestured to the kitchen.

'If it's about paying for the work . . . ?'

'It's not about the work,' Dennis said. His fingers drummed the back of the tablet. 'I need to show you something.'

All this time he'd had his eyes on me. But as Mum stood up, I saw him check the picture of Dad again, and suddenly I knew why the albums were untidy. He knew I'd been stalling when he'd asked to look through them. It didn't take a massive leap of intelligence to figure out I'd been hiding something – like the DVD, for instance.

'Can I see?' said Josie, following them into the kitchen.

I heard Mum say, 'What part of private don't you understand?'

But by then, the movie must have been running. I heard Josie stifle a gasp and knew she was looking at Dad in that chair, reliving another life.

For whatever reason, Dennis was exposing my family to the truth.

And Harvey was alert to it. *Oh, just when I was getting settled.*

He performed a minor reality shift and we materialised at the kitchen door.

Josie had both hands clamped across her mouth. Mum was shaking her head in disbelief. Dennis knew right away that the Michael in the doorway was not the kid he'd talked bikes and football and aliens with, though something alien was staring at him now. In an instant, the tablet flew out of his hands and crashed against the kitchen wall, cracking the face of the clock that hung there.

'Josie, Darcy, get out of the house!' he shouted.

He set his hands for a fight, but how could he take on the might of dragons?

Just as on the terraces at Churston Vale, Harvey performed another shift and threw Dennis backwards, this time with enough force to send him through the kitchen window. Dennis landed on the lawn in a crumpled heap, glass all around him, a trail of blood running out of his mouth. Josie paddled her feet and screamed. Mum, equally terrified, just kept on saying, 'Michael . . . ? Michael . . . ?'

Harvey made me look at her.

My hand went forward and gripped her throat.

In my head, I was yelling at Harvey to stop, but his will was too strong, his control too great.

'Sleep,' he said, and Mum collapsed where she stood.

He turned on Josie. She was red-eyed and whimpering, effervescent with fear. She bolted for the front room, but Harvey slammed the door before she could get there. She tore a calendar off the wall and hurled it at me. Tried the same with a host of fridge magnets. Kicked a stool across my path. All pointless.

'What have you done?' she sobbed. She pressed herself against the wall and looked down at Mum. 'What are you? What have you done to Dad?'

The doorbell rang again.

Josie gasped, knowing this was her chance. She tried to call out, but Harvey had my hand across her mouth in a flash. A moment later, she was on the kitchen floor as well.

*Time to go*, said Harvey.

He marched me to the front door and made me open it.

'You ready?'

Will Reynard was on the step, dressed as though he was ready to go bowling: turned-up jeans, checked shirt, grey jacket. Blue loafer shoes. He glanced over my shoulder into the hall, saw that everything was calm and ordered.

'Yeah,' I said.

He nodded at Dennis's truck. 'Company?'

'The roofer. Here to finish some plastering. Mum's taken the morning off work. She's upstairs getting Josie ready for school.'

Reynard nodded slowly. He glanced once more into the house. 'Okay, let's go.'

I stepped out, shutting the door behind me.

At the car, Harvey said, *Take a good look, Michael.*

He meant at the house. My home for so long.

'Why am I looking?'

The answer was chilling.

*Last time you'll ever see it,* he said.

# 33
## BUNKER

**WHEREVER WE WERE GOING, IT WASN'T TO THE UNICORNE FACILITY. THEIR HQ WAS IN A DISUSED COAL MINE ON THE FAR SIDE OF** Holton, but the car was turning away from there, heading south towards the sea, driving fast.

*Ask them*, said Harvey, still with a stranglehold on my thoughts. I was constantly trying to fight him now. But if I thought about what he'd done in the kitchen, he just filled my head with a band of white noise. In some ways, that was worse than the pain. I had little choice but to obey him.

He forced me to ungrit my teeth and say, 'Where are we going?'

In the absence of Mulrooney, Chantelle was at the

wheel. Agent Reynard was sitting beside me. 'UNICORNE has many sites,' he said. 'We're taking you to one that's a little remote from the main facility. You'll find it interesting, Michael. It's an underground bunker, built just after the Second World War to shelter military command in the event of a nuclear attack.'

'Why are we going there?'

'When you're dealing with something as precious as a piece of dragon scale, you want everything to be secure, don't you?'

'What's going to happen?'

'I'm not entirely sure. I'm not familiar with UNICORNE's neural acceleration programme. I'm only an interested party, remember.'

I looked at Chantelle. She had her gaze fixed firmly on the road.

'All they did with Dad was regress him with hypnosis. Why do we need to be in a nuclear bunker for that?'

Reynard opened his hands. 'You're asking the wrong guy, Michael. Like I said, I'm little more than a casual observer.'

*He's lying*, Harvey said. *This feels like a set-up. Ask him something else and read his eyes.*

'Where's Klimt, anyway?'

He replied calmly, 'Klimt is at the bunker, preparing everything with Preeve.'

Gold flecks sprang up around his pupils. He was telling the truth.

'You sound wary, Michael. Are you having second

thoughts about the procedure?'

The way he said *procedure* chilled me. It didn't help that his stare had turned so intense. He wasn't trying to glamour me, I was sure of that, but I got the impression he was reading me somehow. It made me wonder if he could see flecks as well.

A light flashed on the leather armrest between us. He unhooked a phone and spoke into it quietly. 'Yes, we're in the car now.' He glanced at me again. 'Edgy, but ready, I think. Yes, that would be an affirmative.' He put the phone down. 'The director is pleased that you're—'

'Why did you come after Hartland?' The suddenness of this question surprised me. Harvey was getting a little sloppy, making my voice tone fluctuate. But if Reynard had noticed, he was showing no sign of it.

He held his hands at a modest surrender position. The same hands that had melted the bars of Freya's cage. I instinctively leant back. For the moment, at least, Harvey was allowing me freedom of movement. 'Hartland was a dangerous fugitive. He left a trail of destruction all across New Mexico. He had to be stopped.'

'Captured, you mean. You wanted your guinea pig back in its cage.'

'I mean stopped,' Reynard said, with no inflection in his voice. 'He was out of control.'

'Zone 16's control.'

Reynard smiled and steepled his fingers. 'Some genies are safer in their bottles, don't you think?' He chose his next words with care. 'I realise this is a sensitive issue, you being of similar . . . composition to Hartland, but we're the good guys, Michael. I'm kind of surprised we're having a semantic debate on the subject.'

*Look stupid*, said Harvey. *He won't expect a kid of your age to know what* semantic *means. Screw up your face or he'll know something's wrong.*

He immediately played with my facial muscles. I saw myself reflected in the glass behind Reynard's head. I looked like Quasimodo chewing a wasp. Reynard smiled and glanced at the road ahead.

Chantelle wasn't slowing down. She was either a very confident driver or wasn't expecting to meet other traffic. We were driving through an area of low-lying marshland, thinning out on both sides into wispy sand dunes and patchy vegetation. Every now and then, the car's nose dipped and showed me a glimpse of flat, grey water. We were crossing the Kinver Ness Nature Reserve, a designated wildlife and seabird sanctuary. Dad had brought the family here once to fly kites on the rolling pebbled beach that bridged the gap between the land and the sea. I looked up, half hoping I might see a dragon shape fluttering against the monochrome clouds. To my horror, I saw not a dragon but a crow.

'Freya,' I whispered, before Harvey could stop me.

'What?' said Reynard, turning his head.

Harvey was quickly frying me again. *Do that once more and you'll suffer.*

*Live with it; she's coming for you, Hartland.*

*She thinks I'm dead, you idiot. It's you she's following.*

*No, her senses are better than ours. She'll know you're around me. She won't rest until she has her claws in you. She's looking for payback for Raik.*

Agh.

Pain and white noise.

My head jerked as he brought me under control.

'Michael?' Reynard said. His hand drifted inside his jacket, as if he might be reaching for a weapon.

'I'm okay. Headache.'

'I thought I heard you mention Freya.'

'I was wondering what had happened to her, that's all.'

'She up there?'

Harvey shook my head for me. 'No.'

The car rolled to a stop. 'We are here,' said Chantelle, tapping a touchscreen data display.

Here? Where? We were in the middle of a wilderness. Acres of pebble beach all around us, an immense playground of sea up ahead.

Chantelle backed the car up a few feet, following directional beeps on her screen. 'In position,' she said.

'Okay,' said Reynard, 'take us down.'

The door locks clunked.

Chantelle saw me jump. 'A precaution,' she said. 'Do not panic, Michael.' She tapped an ID code into her screen. Right away, I heard a grinding noise and felt a jolt as the car began to sink. She had parked on some kind of access plate, hidden just under the beach. Pebbles clattered aside as we were drawn down into a man-made shaft. I thought I heard a pebble hit the roof of the car. Either that or . . . I lost track of the thought as a string of neon blue lights came on. The hole we'd created closed above us, shutting out the sky.

We continued to descend for another thirty feet or so. Then I felt a second jolt, and the neon lights dimmed. A pneumatic door seal opened in front of us. For a moment, I thought Chantelle would start the engine and drive straight through. Instead, she opened her door and clicked the locks on mine.

We all got out of the car.

I followed Chantelle on to a steel mezzanine that overlooked a large rectangular room; an underground chamber, in effect, lit by an even, mauve-coloured light. On the left-hand side was a glass control room. Preeve was inside it, his concentration fixed on a sloping console that looked like a studio mixing desk. He dipped his head towards a microphone. 'They're here.'

Klimt was sitting with his back to us, in a large black chair in the middle of the floor. He swung it around to face the mezzanine wall. The chair looked like standard office issue, padded leather on a swivel base. But as we came down the stairs and Klimt rose to greet us, I saw it was fitted with electrical contacts and a cradle of electrodes at the upper wings.

Nothing like that had been on the chair I'd seen on the DVD.

'Hello, Michael. I trust you had an . . . uneventful journey?'

Klimt and Reynard exchanged a glance. I tried to look

back at the mezzanine level, wondering if that clonk I'd heard had been Freya on the roof of the car, but Harvey got hold of me and made me ask, 'What's this?'

He rested my hand on what looked from the back like a rowing boat standing on its stern. There were eight in total, all about head height, spaced around the chair like a ring of standing stones.

Klimt said, 'They are what we call wave posts. When you are ready to proceed, you will sit in the chair and Preeve will initiate all eight posts. They are designed to emit oscillating pulses of microwave energy at wavelengths consistent with the background radiation of the universe. The random interchange of waves will create an infinite web of quantum angles, inducing a gravitational effect that will enable us to—'

'Where's the scale?' Harvey made me butt in. He couldn't have been more blunt if he'd come out and said, *Cut the* Doctor Who *crap*.

Klimt did that rare thing for him: he smiled. 'Preeve, would you light the floor area, please?'

'We're not ready,' the scientist muttered, his voice echoing over the sound system.

'Doctor, do as I say,' Klimt said, not taking his eyes off me for a moment.

I looked for Reynard. He had gone into the control room to stand by Preeve. Chantelle was with him. It reminded me of the way dentists and their nurses stand away from the chair whenever they take an X-ray of teeth. 'Show it,' I heard Reynard say quietly to Preeve.

Preeve sighed and threw a few switches. The entire floor area under the chair quickly lit up. My father's body was floating horizontally in a glass tank approximately three feet deep, filled with pale blue fluid. Anyone unfamiliar with UNICORNE technology might have thought he was dead or drowning. But I'd been in a similar fluid myself and knew that it was warm and breathable. Liam Nolan had described it to me once as water supersaturated with an isotope of oxygen and life-supporting nutrients. In this light, it looked strangely like the stuff I'd seen Klimt drink from time to time, but there was no room in my head to think about that now. All I could focus on was Dad. He was naked, apart from a cloth around his waist. A tangle of fine brown fibres grew out of his fingertips and toes, weaving around him like wicker. In the centre of his chest was the dragon scale I'd seen in the artefact room, surgically grafted on to his skin.

*Interesting,* said Harvey.

*What have they done?* I mouthed in panic. To get the scale now, Harvey would have to rip Dad's chest apart.

Klimt said, 'Ah, the Mleptra are active. That is good.'

In the tank with Dad were dozens of the strange octopus creatures. They weren't busy around him as I'd seen them be before, but were static in the way that stars in space appear to be motionless. As I drew close, they started to twinkle and a few changed colour. Tiny pulses of light began to shoot around the network of fibres.

'They have detected the implant inside you,' said Klimt. 'Congratulations, Michael. You have made a small but important connection. Phase one of the experiment is therefore successful.'

'Then let's move on to phase two,' I almost growled.

And Harvey forced me past Klimt and into the chair.

'Power it up. I'm ready.'

## 34
### ESCAPE
••••••••••

'VERY WELL,' SAID KLIMT. 'FIRST, YOU WILL
NEED TO BE RESTRAINED.'
'WHAT?' I INSTINCTIVELY CLENCHED A FIST.

He stepped forward regardless. 'You saw on the DVD
of your father that the procedure can cause the subject to
become animated. No matter what happens, you need to
stay in the chair at all times.'

He picked up my unclenched hand and put it, palm
down, on a pad at the end of the armrest. It lit up green
around my fingers. I felt my fingers sink into it slightly as
if I'd pressed my hand into modelling wax.

*Don't worry about the restraints*, said Harvey. *Once they
activate the system, nothing will hold us.*

*What about Dad? How are you going to get the scale*

*without—?*

More white noise.

*Just play their game and I'll give you your dad.*

Klimt put my other hand in place. Two clamps then came over each arm, one at the wrist, one above the elbow. He put his fingers on my temples and eased me right back into the chair. As soon as the back of my head touched the rest, the cradle of electrodes came together like spiders' legs. I flinched as I felt them 'walking' on my skin.

'Do not be concerned,' he said. 'The electrodes are detecting your cranial nerves. It will only take moments. Once they are in place and Preeve opens the channels, you will be directly connected to the scale. I will then guide you through the rest of the process.'

I looked down at the fluid-filled tank. Harvey allowed me to ask, 'Why have you fused the scale to Dad's skin?'

Klimt stepped outside the circle of posts. I swivelled the chair so I could follow him. 'I have some information I must share with you, Michael. It concerns your father's condition and will explain what I am about to show you. Do not be afraid. Your life is about to change for the better.' He tapped a small keypad on the wall, and two huge panels drew back. It was dark behind the panels, but I could make out the shape of one of the weird pods they'd put me in once when I'd been in their lab. The pods looked like those sarcophagus things you see in the Egyptian rooms of museums, but this one had a curved glass lid, and pipework and cables springing out of the sides. If I was expecting to see a mummified pharaoh, I was way off track. Klimt ordered Preeve to bring up the lights. There was a figure inside the pod. It was still, but it looked a long way from dead.

A boy, with pale pink skin and soft brown hair.

A perfect clone of me.

*What in creation is this?* said Harvey.

I couldn't have put it better myself.

My heartbeat doubled its rhythm. It was all I could do to keep breathing.

'Preeve,' said Klimt.

With a zing, the wave posts lit. The chair shifted its position a fraction and locked itself in line with the clone. The lighting in the room changed from mauve to dark green. Harvey was really buzzing now, wondering what the heck was going on. There had been nothing like this on the film of Dad.

From the posts came stream after stream of thin blue rays. They lit the chair in a strobing matrix, making it appear to float in mid-air. Bizarrely, I remembered my physics teacher, Mr Churston-Ferrers, showing us a tightly wound ball of string and asking the class to imagine that the crisscrossing lines of string were the pathways made by a single electron whizzing around a nucleus at the speed of light. What would it feel like, he'd asked, to be at the centre of the ball, following that electron with your eyes? Sitting here, I thought I could answer his question: it would feel like floating at the core of a small but perpetually changing universe, as if you were everywhere and nowhere at once, as if you could touch infinity with your mind, as if all creation was yours to control . . .

Klimt turned to face me, moving like a spectre beyond the blur of lines. 'The boy in the pod is an android, Michael. He is semi-organic with a nervous system built on a graphene interface. He has your precise genetic make-up, but his DNA has been modified in two important ways. First, the defective gene that gave rise to your leukaemia has been repaired by the Mleptra. Second, he possesses a fusion of the four chemical bases that make up human DNA with the two extra ones found in the material we were able to extract from the scale. Human DNA consists of two helical strands of these paired chemical bases. The material from the scale has three. If the scale is indeed a dragon relic, then this enhanced genetic configuration is our clearest pointer yet to the source of their powers, chiefly their ability to manipulate the fabric of the universe – to alter reality, as you have done.'

He touched his hand to the pod. At first I assumed he was about to throw a switch to activate the thing. But the way – the almost human way – he spread his fingers made me think he was reaching out to something like family: his android child, his artificial son. I saw a sudden flow of movement along the tubes, and the pod began to fill with blue fluid.

'A few days ago, I made you aware that we had introduced a small amount of the scale into your body. A quantity of Mleptra was added to your bloodstream as well. This was done to improve your medical condition, but it was also an experiment to screen your capacity to control the changes we predicted you would go through. We have been monitoring those changes since you were ten years old. Laboratory tests on the Mleptra have shown that they, through long-term adherence to the scale, have been able to absorb minute quantities of dragon DNA and fuse it into their genetic make-up. The Mleptra are primitive in comparison to humans, but they have one significant advantage over your species: they have been able to stabilise the changes – you have not. Your reality shifts, though deeply impressive, are disturbingly erratic. Do you see what this is leading to?'

I looked at my mirror image in the pod. 'No.'

'You have always wished to know what happened to your father. Shortly, you will learn the truth. Thomas realised, as Jacob Hartland should have realised, that the human mind is too emotionally led to bear the responsibility that comes with inheriting the power to change the universe. That is why he gave his blessing to the only procedure he knew might one day return him to you, when you were old enough to understand.'

'What procedure? I thought you just regressed him and he never came back?'

Klimt looked at me as if he wanted to die. I'd never seen anything so close to human in his purple android eyes before. He looked at the control room and nodded. 'Not quite.'

The chair began to spin, backwards at first, then in a random disorientating manner as it began to pick up speed.

'KLI . . . MMM . . . TTTT!' I screamed. 'WHAT DID YOU DOOOOOO?!'

'Patience,' he said, as if he'd just rebooted his emotional hard drive. 'First, we must rid you of Hartland's influence.'

*What?* I felt Harvey rush to the front of my consciousness.

'Preeve, the tone.'

My head was suddenly filled with a high-pitched whine that raked through my brain at enormous speed. If someone had set off a whisk in my head, it couldn't have been more painfully invasive. I knew why they'd done it – or thought I did. We'd discovered on my previous UFile missions that certain high-pitched sounds vibrated my senses, allowing a 'ghost' form of me to detach from my body. But on this occasion, at this frequency, it wasn't me that peeled away, it was Harvey. I remembered Klimt saying, 'No matter what happens, stay in the chair.' That command kept playing at a subliminal level, somehow embedded in the tone Preeve was sending. *Stay in the chair. Stay in the chair.*

Harvey's 'ghost' wriggled into the matrix and froze. It was nothing but a kind of plasma cloud at first, a peculiar squiggle of goo. Then Preeve changed the tonal frequency, and the plasma squirmed like a flat balloon filling up with air. It morphed into the shape of Jacob Hartland, Zone 16 fugitive.

'Excellent,' I heard Klimt say.

And it was – for a moment. But as the chair continued to whirl, I saw Freya come swooping down from the mezzanine, claws wide, eyes black with vengeance. I screamed at her to stop, fearing she would hit the rays and burn up like a rocket re-entering the atmosphere.

But it was worse, far worse than that.

Her speed of attack took her inside the matrix, where she slowed like a body in water. She came to a halt, still in flight mode, several feet away from Harvey.

One of the wave posts flickered.

Klimt flashed a look towards the control room.

Through the speakers I heard Preeve say, 'God in heaven! The continuum is broken!'

The flickering post went dead.

The matrix faltered.

My chair stopped spinning with a gut-wrenching brake.

The remaining seven posts went dead.

The clamps on my chair defaulted back to the open position.

I spilled out, giddily, on to my knees.

Freya fluttered in confusion and dropped.

Preeve screamed across the airwaves, 'Klimt, I can't hold him!'

Agent Reynard came sprinting out of the control room, a laser weapon in his hand.

He fired at Harvey's ghost but was far too late.

The ghost had disappeared like a light going out.

And by then, the nightmare had truly begun.

The glass tank underneath me exploded.

The chair gave way, taking me down with it.

Blue fluid flooded the bunker, filling the air with a methylated smell.

Mleptra were washed all across the floor.

Preeve called out, 'He's jumped to Thomas! He's in the hive!'

Klimt began to shake like a puppet on strings.

And Jacob Hartland rose again.

This time in the body of my father.

## 35
### HIVE

**IT WAS LIKE THE SET OF A HORROR MOVIE. HARTLAND SAT UP, A TRUE FRANKENSTEIN'S MONSTER, FLEXING HIS HANDS AS IF HE COULD** not quite believe they'd been given life. The fibres growing from his fingertips and toes now clung to his body like sticky brown algae. He tore them off and cast them aside, standing up and stepping on the broken glass as if it were as harmless as sugar grains. The only person he looked at was Klimt. Something had gone seriously wrong with Klimt. He had dropped to one knee with his hands fluttering close to his head. He looked like a TV image on pause. I'd watched a documentary once about how computer-generated images are made by digitising the movements of actors into a wire frame of pixels. That was

Klimt now: a billion points of interlocked light, fizzing with sparks. Hartland stared down at the stricken android like a king might scorn an unworthy peasant. Then he put his head back and laughed, drawing a breath that sounded like a freight train passing through a tunnel. In his hand was a single Mleptra. He crushed it and let its juice trickle through his fingers, then threw the mangled body aside.

Reynard ranged up, gun held double-handed. He was aiming at the scale in the monster's chest. Chantelle was further back, covering him.

'Hartland!'

The monster fixed him with a dead-eyed glare.

I was on my knees, cradling Freya. She was struggling in my hands, screaming at me to let her attack. The boy in the pod was silent, unaffected. I could see no sign of Preeve and guessed he was hiding in the control room.

'Will, don't shoot!' I yelled.

He circled to his right, never taking his eyes off his target. 'Michael, stay clear! This is not your father! I repeat, not your father!'

'Michael . . .' Hartland said in a voice that sounded like Dad just waking from sleep. He put one hand to the scale and ripped it clean away from the skin.

In the hole it left behind was a human heart, surrounded by Mleptra and computer circuitry.

*Aaark!* cried Freya, speaking the words I couldn't. *Lab rat gone wrong*.

So, so wrong.

Hartland roared and threw the scale away, hurling it

with such incredible force that it shattered the glass of the control room. I heard a yelp from inside and saw Preeve scuttle out on his hands and knees.

At that point, Agent Reynard fired.

Somehow, Hartland turned his head quicker than the ray could travel. I'd always been taught that laser light ran straight and true, but the burst that came from Reynard's gun curved away from Hartland's chest and gathered in his palm like a ball of fire. With barely a flick, he hurled it back. It hit the floor in front of Reynard, instantly igniting a pool of the fluid. A wall of bright blue flames leapt up. I saw Mleptra burn and burst. Chantelle yelped as the flare of heat caught her. She and Reynard backed off, shielding their faces.

Hartland turned his attention to Klimt.

Using the hand that had caught the laser beam, he steadied his palm just above Klimt's head. Klimt's body went into a violent spasm. Bolts of energy passed from his eyes, rippling into Hartland's fingertips. In a matter of moments, it was done. Hartland broke the connection and Klimt finally slumped to the floor. He looked 'human' again, but his purple eyes were vacant. Points of light flickered on his body and went out.

'Dad!'

It felt like such a weird thing to say, but I could think of no other way to get Hartland's attention. He turned to face me, blue fluid dripping from the ends of his hair. For one small instant, he *was* my father. He looked and spoke and moved like my father. A father with dragon DNA inside him, and who knew how much artificial body-work?

'Dad, what have they done to you?'

'Thomas Malone has been terminated,' he said, his hand still crackling with residual energy.

'T-terminated? What?'

He glanced down at Klimt. 'The life force has been removed from the android. I am all that remains.'

And before my eyes, he began to transform, into the shape of the Mogollon monster I'd seen on the petroglyph drawings. His hair retracted and his head turned a freaky pear-drop shape, eyes like slanted almonds: alien. He grew taller, slimmer, his elongated arms almost floating at his sides. An extra finger appeared on both hands. His body colour faded to grey.

Through an O-shaped mouth he said, 'When the crow is gone, join me, Michael.'

He turned his fingers. The wave posts came to life again. I let go of Freya, but not quickly enough to get her away. A new matrix formed around her, at a frequency clearly designed to remove anything undead out of existence. For one awful moment, I thought she was going to be taken apart, atom by atom. Then the matrix died again suddenly. Will Reynard had jumped the dying flames and used whatever power he possessed to melt part of a wave post, doing enough to disable the system.

'Preeve, get over here! Now!' He clamped my face in his hands. 'You okay?'

Freya flapped away towards the mezzanine. I nodded.

'Where's Hartland?'

'Gone. Thin air. Disappeared.'

'Chantelle?'

'By the wall, hurt. I've called for backup. Preeve!'

The scientist came towards us, tiptoeing through the broken glass. 'No, no,' he muttered, kneeling by Klimt. 'This can't happen. This just can't *happen*!' He ran a small scanner over the android. 'Wiped. Every meta-organic system erased. The director—'

Reynard wanted none of that. Grabbing the lapels of Preeve's lab coat, he said, 'Stop blabbering about your *toy*. I need to know where Hartland's gone.' He plucked a tablet out of Preeve's pocket. 'Can we pick him up on the security trace? A visual? A heat source? Anything?'

Preeve fumbled one arm of his glasses into place. 'What does it matter? With the hive at his command, he'll be able to move in quantum leaps; the moment we observe him, he could relocate at the speed of light. Going after him is pointless. He's unstoppable. He could eliminate any one of us as easily as rubbing out a pencil drawing.'

'Hive?' Now it was my turn to grab hold of Preeve. I beat his shoulder. 'What do you mean *hive*?' Klimt had used this term once about the Mleptra. 'And what did Hartland mean when he said the life force had been removed from the android? What's happened to Klimt? What did you do to *Dad*?'

'Tell him,' said Reynard, urgently tapping the tablet screen. 'Tell him, Preeve, or I'll rub you out myself.'

Preeve's face turned a sickly shade of vanilla. 'I'd

remind you that you have no jurisdiction here, Reynard.'

The American raised his gun. 'This does.'

Preeve gulped and swept a hand through his hair. He knelt back on his haunches, looking defeated. 'Oh, very well. It hardly matters now. We're all doomed, anyway.' He looked me in the eye. 'Your father came back from New Mexico heavily contaminated by the Mleptra. By the time we realised what had happened, they were too well established in every organ of his body to eradicate or control. So we let them replicate freely. What you saw in the tank wasn't a man but a giant human-shaped culture dish, a storage facility where the Mleptra could be contained and harvested. He's been like that since . . .'

'Since WHAT?' I whacked him again.

'Since he separated, permanently,' Preeve spat back. 'You just don't get this, do you, Malone? You don't have a clue what's happening here. Everything we've done – the implants, the missions, the monitoring of your family – it's all been designed to bring you to this moment. That idiot crow has ruined everything. If she hadn't gate-crashed the matrix, you'd have been the first true hybrid, the perfect synthesis of human, Mleptra, and graphene technology. Now you'll remain exactly as you are, a jaded experiment slowly running out of control. You're going to be the snotty schoolkid who vaporises the world on a whim one day because someone steals his girlfriend or his football team loses. I'll tell you *exactly* what happened to your father. During our experiments with neural acceler-ation, we discovered that certain high-frequency sounds could cause the out-of-body experiences you've had on your missions. We'd always expected the "ghost" to return to the body it had left – until the day we linked Klimt to the neural interface and your father deserted his own body and jumped to the machine he'd helped to design. That's right, Michael. Now you know. Your father was never lost in the multiverse. He was here all along. There was never going to be any search for him. He is, he *was*, Klimt's consciousness. That's what Hartland terminated. And you and your crow have helped him do it!'

**36**

**SWITCH**

**I FELT NUMB. SICK. ANGRY. SO ANGRY. BUT AT LAST, SOME THINGS WERE BEGINNING TO MAKE SENSE, LIKE THE TIME THAT KLIMT HAD VISITED** the house and sat in Dad's favourite chair to talk. I remembered the aching pang I'd felt when I'd watched him solve a Rubik's cube or pick a piece of fluff off the arm of the chair and drop it the way Dad would have done. The worst moment of all was the time I'd seen real sorrow in his eyes when he'd looked into the study and seen the *Tree of Life* painting on the wall. What was going through his circuits then? What had Klimt's high-powered 'interface' made of the artwork Dad had admired so much, the artist he'd named his creation after? Was Dad yearning to come back and be among us then, just like we were desperate to have him home? What had stopped Klimt from revealing his true self to me? Was he afraid I'd reject him? Or that Mum would reject him? Or was his ultra-logical mind simply not human enough to care?

'Why?' I said to Preeve, fighting to keep my temper in check.

'Why what?' he said irritably, looking around. A red warning light was flashing near the control room.

'Why did Klimt crash? Something was wrong with him before Hartland drained him. Why?'

'Preeve, what's with the light?' said Reynard, still working with the tablet, concentrating hard on his search for Hartland.

'He's locked the doors,' Preeve muttered, straightening up like a meerkat. 'Heaven help us, he plans to incarcerate us here.' He got up and stumbled back to the control room.

'Go with him,' said Reynard, heading towards the mezzanine. 'I'll check the exits. And, Michael?'

'Yes?'

He looked down at Klimt. 'I'm sorry – for your loss.'

I wanted to feel sorrow, but couldn't. My head was just a mess of confused loyalties. I nodded silently and ran to the control room. Preeve was bending over the console, throwing switches and levers like a man trying to land a spinning Tardis. 'No, no, no. He can't do that. No. We'll suffocate in minutes.'

'Preeve, tell me: why did Klimt fold?'

He pushed me aside to get at a keyboard. He started hammering what looked like passcodes into it. An alarm now accompanied the flashing lights. One of the computers unhelpfully reported a serious malfunction in the ventilation system.

'Preeve?!'

He pressed his palms down hard on the console. 'Has it escaped your notice that I'm busy here, Michael? Your Mogollon friend, wherever he is, has thrown some kind of reality shift, closing down the bunker's peripheral systems. That means no one can get in and no one can get out, and in approximately' – he looked up at a screen – 'six minutes and thirty-seven seconds we're all going to be gasping for air. In short, we're about to die in here.'

'If I'm going to die, I want to know the truth. Why did you keep Dad in that state? It's gross. Surely you could have farmed the Mleptra somewhere else?'

He whipped off his glasses to read a monitor. 'It's not as simple as that. Despite your father's consciousness switch, Klimt could never quite make the break from Thomas. There was some kind of quantum entanglement between them that somehow involved the Mleptra as well. That's why Klimt was always drinking their juice. It seemed to be a kind of . . . battery acid for him. If we tried to stop Thomas's life support or relocate the Mleptra, Klimt began to malfunction. It was as if an invisible cord was holding them together.'

'Who was in control? Dad or the machine?'

'Good question,' he muttered.

'You mean you don't *know*?'

'It was an interdependent relationship, Michael. Only Klimt could truly say how it worked.'

'How do you know Dad wasn't trying to break free?'

'*What?*'

'How do you know he intended to jump in the first place? What if the machine took over and stole Dad's consciousness during those regression experiments?'

'No, no, no. That's . . . preposterous. Anyway, your father *agreed* to the procedure.'

'You were there? You heard him?'

'No, not in . . .' He paused and thought about this. 'I . . . The director . . .' He paused again.

'The Bulldog. *He* set it up?'

Preeve stared into the middle distance.

'He tricked you, didn't he? Tricked us all. So he could create the perfect android.'

'Look, I don't have time for this. What's done is done. Your father's gone. I can't bring him back. When Hartland took control of the hive, it would have caused massive neural feedback. Klimt – Thomas – never stood a chance.'

From the mezzanine, Reynard shouted, 'Preeve, I've got zero response on the door seals!'

'Tell me something I *don't* know,' the scientist muttered. He dropped into a chair and slid sideways towards a bank of equipment winking with all sorts of warning lights. He tried button after button. 'Dead, dead, dead. Can't even get a wireless link.'

'What about the scale? Where does that come into it?'

He rubbed his eyes, wearied by the constant buzz of questions. 'This has never been about the scale. What we call the artefact is dried-out matter we can't identify. Some kind of toughened skin, certainly. But dragon? You might as well call it dodo rind. We let you go on believing it was dragon because it suited us to. We've never been able to conclusively prove that human proximity to the scale yields any consistent or reproducible effects, though it does seem to adapt better to some subjects more than others.'

'Like me, you mean. It works in me.'

'To some extent, yes, but we've never established a coherent mechanism. The Mleptra, on the other hand, can be readily observed, engineered and measured. The scale has some influence, certainly, but in my opinion, the Mleptra are the primary source of your powers. You heard what Klimt said. They get inside a host's cellular network and attempt to "improve" the genetic model. Much of what they do is benign and helpful, but the symbiosis with humans is vague and unpredictable – your reality shifts being a case in point. Hence the need to control the creatures with a cognitive system based on logic.' He slid the chair back my way. 'Might be able to bypass the auxiliary grid if . . .'

'Why did you put the scale on Dad's chest?'

He dipped under the console and ripped out a wire. 'To keep Hartland in the game.'

'You knew he was inside me?'

'Does a bee make honey? Of course we knew. We have

a database full of your behavioural patterns. The blips in your temperament were plainly caused by a secondary stimulus and not your usual tedious hormonal outbursts. Reynard confirmed it on the journey here. He reads flecks, like you.'

More wires came out.

'Why did he throw the scale away?'

'Ow! What?' He banged his head on the desk as he emerged.

'You said the scale adapts to some people more than others. Did it reject Hartland? Why didn't it have any power for him?'

Preeve sighed and pressed his fingers to his eyelids. 'Your average roof tile has more power than the piece of debris Hartland disposed of. What you saw on Thomas was a replica of the scale. We did it to mislead Hartland. It was a ruse, Michael. Do you know about ruses?'

Oh, I knew about ruses all right. I'd lived with them since the day I'd joined UNICORNE. Mention of roof tiles made me think about the scene at home. I was pretty sure Harvey hadn't killed Mum or Josie, and Dennis had been moving when he'd hit the grass, but I needed to get back to them as soon as I could. What's more, I knew a way out of the bunker, one that Preeve hadn't even considered. When the moment came, I could alter my reality and get us to safety, but not before I had the answers I wanted. 'Tell me about the film. If the scale is useless, why did Dad regress into dragon times? He wasn't faking. I know he wasn't. I heard him speak their language. *Galan aug scieth.'*

'Oh, fol-de-rol-de-rol,' Preeve snorted. 'There, I've sung a song in the language of unicorns! I didn't say the scale was useless, just erratic. And testimonies taken under hypnosis are notoriously unreliable. What that idiot, Nolan, captured on camera was your father's decline into Wonderland. There was never any proof he'd connected with the past.'

'But his skin changed. He started to transform.'

Preeve scratched his forehead. Pearls of sweat were beginning to gather. He fumbled his glasses back on. 'I agree, that was an interesting moment. But we could find no trace of transmutation, despite rigorous testing of your father's blood and dermal tissues. Conclusion: it was a stress reaction, just like the one I'm having now.'

'No,' I said, 'the change was real. Harvey talked about dragons being able to transform and I've already done it with the crows. And what about that time at Three Rivers? Dad had barely touched the scale before it allowed him to escape from the helicopters. That means he had a strong connection to it. What if me and Dad are related to someone in the past who had real dragon auma and that's why the scale works better for us?'

'This is ridiculous,' Preeve said, flapping his hands like a frightened bird. 'I don't have time for your poppycock theories. In fact, I don't have time for—'

'Got him!'

We turned our heads and saw Reynard come clattering down the mezzanine steps. He burst into the control room. 'Hartland's still here.' He zoomed an image on the tablet. The Mogollon creature that had once been my father was standing on the pebble beach, facing the sea. 'He's playing something. Looks like a flute.'

'Sounding our death tune,' Preeve muttered glumly.

'He's calling me,' I said. 'The flute's a kind of in-joke. I need to go out there. Preeve, where's the scale?'

He threw aside the wires he'd removed from the console. 'We're finished, boy. Accept it. Say your prayers.'

I whizzed his chair around, making his glasses skew across his face. 'No. I can alter my reality and keep us alive. But I can do much more if I have the scale.'

'More?' said Reynard.

I checked the countdown. One minute forty-eight seconds remaining. 'I'm going out to face Hartland, to finish this – for good.'

Reynard nodded. 'Okay, but take me with you.'

'No. No way.'

'Michael, he's strong. You can't do this alone.'

'I can,' I said, looking into his eyes. 'I'll form a reality in which you're safe, but I have to deal with Hartland myself. He's hurt or killed nearly everyone close to me. This is personal, Will. And you don't have time to argue.'

He pressed his lips into a thin straight line. 'All right. Preeve, do as he says.'

Preeve had put his glasses into their case and was neatly folding the lens cloth that cleaned them. It made me think that if he'd had a coffin, he would have been closing the lid on himself. 'You expect me to unravel ten years of research in less time than it would take to boil an egg?'

Reynard grabbed his lapels again. 'I'll crack your head like an egg if you don't start talking. Where's the scale?'

Preeve batted him off. 'There's a segment in the clone, but it's hardwired into the cranium. You'd never get it out in time.'

'A segment?' I asked.

'A piece much larger than your micro implants. If you're right about your dragon ancestors, you'd have been quite the superstar.'

Reynard looked through the shattered window at the pod, where the clone still lay completely motionless. 'If we can't get it out, can we get Michael in?'

'In?' said Preeve.

'The consciousness switch? Can it be done without the technology?'

'Are you serious?' Preeve blustered.

'I have fifty-three seconds of air,' said Reynard. 'I'd say that makes me pretty darned serious. Can it be *done*?'

Preeve checked his readouts. 'Technically, yes. The pathways to the clone are on a different loop from the rest of the equipment. We could use the tone to separate Michael's consciousness, then reverse the neuromagnetic transmitters to encourage his connection to the android. But it's ludicrous to try. There are so many imponderables. It would be like walking a tightrope in ice skates. Any hint of uncertainty could leave him literally lost in the ether. And coming back . . .'

His words tailed off. I took that to mean there would

be no coming back.

'Do it,' I said.

Reynard nodded at Preeve.

'Reynard, think about this,' Preeve hissed. 'If the clone is separated from our control, the fate of the universe will be in his hands. Even if he defeats Hartland, we're literally at his mercy.'

'Then I guess we'll just have to trust him, won't we?'

Preeve gulped and handed me a set of headphones. 'You'd better sit down.'

'One thing,' said Reynard.

The clock was ticking. Nineteen seconds. 'What?'

'Freya. She was flapping at a grille on the mezzanine wall. I sprang it for her. She's in the air ducts somewhere.'

Trying to get out. Trying to get to Hartland. She just would not give up.

'Thanks for the tip-off.' I put the headphones on.

'This will happen very fast,' said Preeve, flicking switches quicker than Josie could text. 'Even in the ghost state, you'll have little time to think. Keep your mind focused on the clone or you'll be vapour.'

'He'll make it,' said Reynard, clamping my shoulder. 'Last words of advice, kid: be strong, be definite and most of all be kind.'

He nodded at Preeve to play the tone.

In an instant, I was out of my body. Preeve was right about the speed of transition. I barely had time to look at the pod before I felt myself speeding towards it.

Bang. Everything went dark for a moment. When I

opened my eyes again, I was in the pod, immersed in fluid.

*Systems active*, my brain seemed to say.

Transfer complete.

Michael Malone reborn.

An android.

**37**
**STATUE**

**THE POD DRAINED OF FLUID AND THE LID SPRANG OPEN. I THOUGHT I WOULD SPLUTTER AND GASP FOR AIR, BUT MY ARTIFICIAL** circuits simply noted the change in the oxygen levels and adjusted my breathing accordingly. I stepped out semi-naked, wet from the fluid but drying fast. On the far side of the bunker, in the control room, I saw Will Reynard holding his throat. At that point, my memory banks kicked in and I remembered why I'd jumped. Instantly, like a car slipping out of a bend and engaging traction control, the threat of danger triggered a whole new sense of what my body was capable of. The opportunity to shift reality and escape the hazard was no longer a wild card but simply the most presentable and sensible option.

Unlike previous danger moments when I might have panicked and anything could have happened, my logic filters assessed the situation and I calmly imagined an alternative reality in which the air vents were open but the door locks closed. In a jolt it was done. The warning lights stopped flashing. The alarms cut off. I saw Reynard and Preeve taking gulps of air. As Reynard looked up, I closed my eyes again and pictured myself on the wasteland outside, fully clothed and fifty feet from Hartland.

The flute playing stopped. He stretched out his hand, the grey arm floating like the tail of a kite. The flute changed into a barren twig. He dropped it and turned around.

'What took you so long?' His voice was harsh and alien, shaped by the perfect O of his mouth.

'Stuff to do. Major refit.'

He tilted his pear-shaped head.

'Isn't this just typical?' I said. 'You wait a few millennia for the perfect android and then two come along at once. Only this one's stronger than the one you "terminated".'

'You sound threatening, Michael. I thought we were allies?'

A cold wind skittered across the pebbles.

'That was before you wiped out my father and tried to tear Freya apart.'

'The crow lives? You saved her?'

'Reynard did. Any moment now, she'll find her way out of the bunker's air vents. She'll want to claw your freaking eyes out, but this is strictly between you and me.'

I blinked. In the space beside us, a life-size tree grew out of the pebbles, the image of the one in the *Tree of Life* painting. On the branch where the single black bird would have sat, I had pictured Freya with a white-tipped tail.

*Aaar-raark?!* she cried, appearing there. Michael, what's happening? Why can't I fly?

Her feet were firmly attached to the branch, exactly the way I'd imagined it.

'This is folly,' said Hartland. 'Why do you protect her? I control the hive. You cannot defeat me.'

Stipples of light began to fall on the pebbles. Hartland glanced at the tree to see dozens of glinting crowns, sprouting like blossoms in the patchwork swirl of branches.

'Take your pick,' I said. 'Each of them represents a different way to die.'

The taunt angered him. 'You think you're the only one capable of tricks?'

He sucked in through his mouth and a gale ripped through the *Tree of Life*, scattering the crowns in a blizzard far across the pebbles. Strands of loose algae left by the tide rose up and dragged them down under the rocks.

But when it was done and the wind had dropped, one crown clinked gently across the stones and came to rest halfway between us. Purple-coloured dragons ran around its rim. A black crow feather skirted the breeze and landed within the circle.

'Good choice,' I said.

I looked up into the barren sky.

The cry of a lone crow grazed the wilderness.

'A crow?' said Hartland.

'The flock,' I said. Dozens were appearing, from all directions.

*Ark!* screamed Freya, beating her ever-restless wings.

But I would not let her leave the tree.

'What are crows against *me*?' said Hartland. And he raised his hand and sent a bolt of energy through the air, making it fork and fork again to catch every approaching bird.

They lit blue and silver, silver and blue. But I was shifting their reality at quantum speed and they kept on coming, a rain of black.

'Listen to their call,' I said calmly.

*Arrk-ark-raark! Galan aug scieth.*

I am you and you are me.

Two birds collided in mid-air.

But they did not fall or break a wing; they merged into one bird. One bigger crow.

Again and again it happened. And those that had merged, merged again with others, until the few that remained came screaming their terrible vengeance on Hartland – and finally merged with me.

By then, I was already transforming. I had called upon the ultimate power of the scale, naming one intention only. Into that intention I poured all the love I had for my father, all the sorrow I felt for my mother, all my commitment to do what was right by Freya and Raik and the rest of their flock. And so, with unflinching conviction, it happened. I made myself turn beyond the shape of a bird and into the body of a fearful dragon.

Hartland backed away, his transparent thoughts reaching into the multiverse, seeking a corner where he might hide. But he was mine to hold, to bind to the stones. Amadeus Klimt had been right about one thing: I was forty times more powerful than Hartland to begin with, forty thousand times more powerful now. With the strength of my mind alone, I reached right into the monster's body and called out the Mleptra. They spilled from its mouth and ears and eyes, and appeared as blooms all over its skin. I called a tide of water from the distant sea and sent the Mleptra into the ocean, to do good among the sentient creatures there. And as Hartland turned to run from me, I reclaimed the dragon auma from him. I opened my jaws and blew a ravaging fire, a fire that turned his bones to ash but his skin to stone, leaving him a statue, hollow in the wilderness, looking forever at the grey horizon, looking for something he would never see.

And when it was done, I released the crows and set myself for one more shift of reality. One final act of strength and kindness that would exhaust every scrap of power I possessed, and in its wake bring closure to all concerned.

I called upon the scale and transformed again.

And when *this* was done, the world was still, the *Tree of Life* gone, the grey skies calm.

Freya was in flight and I was with her.

But this was just a small part of the change.
The rest was at home, still waiting to be seen.
*Ark!* I cried and we circled inland.
North again.
To Holton.

## 38
### REBIRTH
· · · · · · · · · · ·

**WE LANDED TOGETHER ON THE ROOF OF THE GARAGE, DISTURBING NO ONE IN THE GARDEN BELOW. THE SUN WAS OUT, THE KITCHEN DOOR** open. Lavender flourished tall in the borders, pansies fluttered in the window boxes. Josie and Melody were playing on the lawn, blowing soap bubbles at one another. Chantelle came out of the kitchen, carrying a tray of soft drinks in tall glasses, pigtail straws curling out of each one. She was wearing a plain white blouse and a pair of blue jeans that ended in a cutaway V at her calves.

She climbed two steps to the patio area and put the tray down on a table shaded by a wide green umbrella. Adam Mulrooney was sitting beneath it, relaxing in a pale blue T-shirt and shorts. He was talking to Will Reynard, who was wearing a beige linen suit, a folded newspaper on his lap.

'Girls, your lemonade,' Chantelle said.

Melody turned towards the table. 'Uncle Adam, look at this one!' She wafted a giant bubble his way.

Mulrooney pulled a straw from a glass. He sucked it dry, then used it to blow the bubble even higher.

It floated towards the garage, a fragile sphere of purples and greens. It popped in front of Freya. She shook a droplet of soap off her beak.

Melody clapped for joy. 'The birdie popped it, Uncle Adam.'

'Much to its surprise, by the look of it,' he said.

Reynard smiled. 'You get many of those? Crows?'

Mulrooney took a sip of his lemonade and nodded. 'They nest in the trees all along the lane.'

'Interesting birds. I always think there's more to them than meets the eye.'

'I like them,' said Josie. She cupped a hand above her eyes and turned our way. She was wearing a summer dress and looked so pretty. Her freckled arms were tanned, her hair a little longer than usual.

Mulrooney pulled a ringing phone from his pocket.

'Is that them?' Josie gasped.

Mulrooney put the phone to his ear and nodded. 'Hi, where are you? Okay, cool. I'll meet you in the drive. No, we're in the garden, guzzling your lemonade. Yeah, Will's here. His flight leaves at five. Yep. Sure thing. See you soon, buddy.' He cut the call and stood up. 'They're at

Poolhaven crossroads.'

'How long?' asked Josie, knocking her fists together in excitement.

'Five minutes, tops,' Reynard said.

Josie dashed into the house, shouting, 'Camera!'

'I'll bring them through when they arrive,' Adam said. He followed Josie inside.

*Ark?* went Freya. What now?

*Wait*, I said. *Watch.*

'My ribbon's come undone,' Melody whined, dangling the band in front of Chantelle.

'Oh, here, let me see,' Chantelle said kindly. She lifted Melody on to her lap and gathered her soft brown hair into a bunch. As she tied the ribbon, Reynard said, 'When are you back at school?'

'The day after tomorrow.'

'Looking forward to it?'

'*Oui.*' The word followed the slightest of shrugs.

Reynard ran a finger round the rim of his glass. 'Do I detect a slight "*mais*"?'

She nodded. 'I would rather be going with Adam.'

'To the Arctic? Seriously?'

'*Oui.* Why not?'

'What's ar-tick?' asked Melody, kicking her feet.

'A very, very cold place,' Chantelle said, tying the ribbon off in a bow.

'Colder than the *fridge*?'

'MUCH colder than the fridge.' She rubbed Melody's arms.

'Why does Uncle Adam want to go *there*?'

'To see bears,' said Chantelle. She crossed her arms around Melody's waist and rocked her gently from side to side. 'He is going to make films of them and show them on the TV. You like bears, don't you?'

Melody nodded, her head moving like a ball on springs. 'Shall I lend Uncle Adam my reindeer hat?'

'Oh, absolutely,' Reynard said. 'I'd pay good money to see him behind a camera in that.'

Chantelle kissed the top of Melody's head. 'Go and tell Uncle Adam I love him and that he has to wrap up warm for those bears.'

'All right,' said Melody. She scooted inside.

'Sweet,' said Reynard.

'A treasure,' Chantelle agreed. 'So,' she raised her bare feet on to a chair, 'what about you, also off on a lengthy journey? Indonesia this time. Are you going to tell me why?'

He smiled and took a mouthful of lemonade. 'Let's just say it's warmer than the Arctic.'

She kicked his shin gently. 'Always so evasive. What kind of foster brother will not speak to his beautiful sister about his work?' She put on a pair of designer glasses. They were the colour of dark chocolate and the size of small plates. 'What are you, I wonder? Secret agent? Travelling magician? Evil genius? Alien visitor?'

He stirred his lemonade with his straw. 'I've told you before what I do.'

'Unicorn hunter is not an answer.'

'It will be — the day I find one.' He graced her with a lazy smile.

Chantelle slid forwards, stretching her elegant painted toes. 'Indonesia,' she mused, flexing her foot. 'What do I know about Indonesia?'

'They harbour dragons — the Komodo variety.'

Freya shook her feathers and shuffled a claw's width closer to me.

'You have seen them, the lizards?'

'Walked among them — on holiday. A tip: never get too close to a Komodo. Some of those bad boys are ten feet long and can take you out with a single bite, though you might not know it for a couple of weeks. You should go. Adam would be up for that. Being in Komodo National Park is like stepping right back into the Jurassic.'

She drew her left foot closer to examine her nails. 'So now I ask myself, is that what you are: a crazy scientist, cloning dinosaurs?'

He laughed and sipped some air through his teeth. 'Darn it, you got me.'

She flicked his shin again, then leant round to study his face more closely. 'Oh my God, you are not entirely lying.'

'I am,' he said, looking straight at her.

'*Non*. This trip is not a holiday, is it?'

'Drink your lemonade, sis. You're disturbing the crows.'

But Chantelle was buzzing now. 'Tell me something. Anything at all. I promise on my life I will not reveal it.'

Sunlight swept across the garden. Reynard dipped into

his jacket and also put on a pair of dark glasses. They made him look what Mum would call casually handsome. 'Anything?'

'*Oui*.'

He pointed to a planter. 'The daffodils have lasted well this year.'

For that, she punched him. A jab to the shoulder, nothing hard.

'Hey . . . ?'

'Serves you right for being mean.'

'I'm not being mean. I'm being . . .'

'What, Will? What are you being?'

'Protective,' he said, drawing in his lips.

Chantelle picked up a cushion and hugged it. 'Are you trying to frighten me now?'

'If I was, it would be for your own good, trust me.'

'Then go,' she said with a petulant sniff. 'Leave by the rear gate. Sneak away. Do what you do best, William, fall from the sky, then melt like a snowflake. Be gone. Leave us. Who will miss you?'

'Now you're being silly.'

'And you are still being *mean*.'

He slid his glass back and forth along the table, shaking his head on the final push. 'If I did tell you something, how would you know I was telling the truth?'

'I would know,' she said.

Inside the house, a dog began to bark. Will glanced at his watch, and then at the kitchen. 'All right. One time. For your ears only. This is what I do: I travel the world investigating paranormal mysteries. There's a man in Indonesia, crazy scientist type, who claims to have discovered a new species of marine mollusc – a small octopoidal creature, mauve in colour, that lives parasitically under the fins of large cetaceans. He believes these things are alien to our oceans and that they're recent visitors here. He thinks they can communicate telepathically with humans. He hopes they might be used to cure dementia.'

The barking grew louder, more enthusiastic. Voices began to drift into the garden.

'Telepathic molluscs?'

He put his newspaper on the table. 'Is it any weirder than a bulldog setting off to swim the English Channel?' He pointed to an article he'd been reading. 'It drowned,' he added.

Chantelle stood up and moved towards the kitchen. 'I do not believe you.'

'I didn't expect you to,' he said.

'But I think I know what you truly are.'

He opened his hands, inviting an answer.

'An inventor of worlds, a word thief,' she whispered.

'Word thief? That's new.'

*Writer*, she mouthed.

He raised his glass of lemonade. 'I'll drink to that.'

'Trace, come on,' Mulrooney said, ushering a husky out into the garden.

*Theirs?* asked Freya.

*Ark!* A gift.

Trace twirled on the lawn like a grey-and-white firework. She ran to Dennis the moment he set foot in the garden. 'Hey, girl,' he said, offering his hand. He put his free arm around Chantelle and kissed her cheek. She responded with an air kiss, but was quickly consumed with the next person out.

'Oh, he is so BEAUTIFUL!' she gushed.

Out came Mum, with a baby in her arms.

She looked tired, but radiant, and so very proud. Her hair was down and a little wild. She was wearing a loose grey sweater that somehow seemed to work as a wrap for the baby.

'May I hold him for a moment?' Chantelle begged.

'Be my guest.' Mum handed the baby over.

'Oh, look at his little hat,' Chantelle purred, turning him out of the sun's bright glare.

Dennis stepped on to the patio. He clamped hands with Reynard. 'Good to see you, Will. Glad you could make it.'

'Congratulations,' Will said. 'A boy. You must be thrilled.'

'Not *too* thrilled,' said Josie. She was buzzing around, snapping pictures on her tablet. 'Girls rule in this house. Chantelle, smile.'

Dennis laughed and hoisted Melody on to his hip. 'How about you, princess? What do you think of your new baby brother? Do you like him?'

Melody nodded. 'Daddy, the birdies are watching.' She aimed a finger at the garage roof.

'So they are,' he said, looking up. He'd shaved his beard

and looked younger for it.

'They've been there for a while,' Reynard said. 'Like wise men in feathers, following a star.' Smiling, he added, 'I didn't invite them.'

Dennis touched a finger to Melody's nose. 'Are they scaring you, sweetheart?'

She shook her head.

'Are you sure? Do you want me to shoo them off?'

'No,' she said, and leant her head on his shoulder.

'Darcy, come and sit down,' said Adam. He guided Mum over to one of the chairs. 'Drink?' He lifted the lemonade jug.

'I'm fine,' she said, touching his arm.

'He has such incredible eyes,' said Chantelle, rocking the baby in the cradle of her arms. 'Is it me or is the left one lighter than the other?'

'They're officially blue,' said Mum, 'but the left has a definite hint of violet. Dennis, what's wrong with Trace?'

The dog was sitting on the lawn, pricking her ears towards me and Freya. She tilted her head and whined quietly.

'I think those crows are upsetting her,' he said. He put Melody on a chair and clapped his hands at us.

Freya lifted a wing.

*Not yet*, I said. *It isn't time.*

Chantelle gave the baby back to Mum. 'What have you called him?'

'We're still deciding,' said Mum. 'They had me listening to Mozart during the birth, so Dennis thinks we ought to call him Wolfgang.'

'Costly on a football shirt,' said Adam.

'Amadeus would be cheaper,' Reynard suggested, still running with the Mozart theme.

Freya tightened her claws.

'No, it will be plain and simple,' said Mum. 'I have a name in mind. It's only just come to me.'

Before she could reveal it, Chantelle piped up. 'My mother used to say you should name a child by what you hope it will grow up to be.'

'Pelé?' Adam said.

The idea made Dennis laugh.

'Who's Pelé?' Josie asked.

'Famous Brazilian football star,' said Adam.

Josie huffed. 'My brother's not going to play boring football. I'm going to take a picture of those crows.' She moved across the garden to stand by Trace.

'I have some suggestions for what he might be,' Chantelle said. And she reeled off the list she'd thrown at Will: secret agent, travelling magician, evil genius (that one received boos). At the last moment, she swapped alien visitor in favour of . . . 'unicorn hunter'.

A chill breeze blew across the garden.

Adam steadied the patio umbrella.

On the lawn, Trace mewled and got to her feet.

'What *is* the matter with that dog?' Mum said. 'Where's Michael, by the way?' She looked at Will.

'Riding his bike – with a "friend",' he said.

Mum twitched an inquisitive eyebrow.

'Just the messenger,' he said, raising his hands in surrender.

*It's time*, I said to Freya. *Ready?*

She tipped her beak. *Ark!*

On the lawn, Josie stamped her foot. 'Dad, there's something wrong with my camera. I took a picture of the crows, but it's just . . . roof.'

They all looked up as the back gate opened.

Trace barked and turned a circle.

Josie blinked.

'This is Freya,' I said. We stood side by side, holding our bikes at our hips. 'I've brought her around to see the baby.' I plucked a small crow feather off her sweater.

Mum moved a hair off the baby's brow. She looked at Freya as if she might have met her in a previous life. 'Hello, Freya. Would you like some lemonade?'

Freya shook her head. She looked pale, a little frightened. She nodded at the baby. 'What's his name?'

Dennis moved up behind Mum and ran a hand lovingly over her shoulder. 'You said just now you had a name, love.'

'Yes, I like Thomas,' Mum said quietly. 'What do you think, Michael?'

I nodded. 'It's cool.'

Freya shuddered. A glassy tear ran down her cheek.

'Thomas,' said Reynard, raising his drink.

'Thomas,' we agreed, saluting Mum.

Trace wagged her tail.

Mulrooney nodded.

'I s'pose it's better than Pelé,' Josie said with a sniff.

Mum smiled and held the youngster up to the sky. 'Thomas, the unicorn hunter,' she said. 'Why not? Stranger things have happened . . .'

## AUTHOR'S NOTE

This has been quite a journey. A journey into the unknown. I've made no secret of the fact that the UNICORNE Files was inspired by the TV series *The X-Files*. I like to think that Fox Mulder, the hero of those programmes, would have been in his element if asked to investigate cases of cellular memory, telekinesis, and in this story, the mysteries of dragons. Dragons have fascinated me for the past fifteen years, ever since I picked up a clay model one day and introduced it into a book that eventually became known as *The Fire Within*. Since that time, I've been asking myself one important question about dragons – a question that has had some interesting ramifications. The question is simple enough – well, simple enough to ask: *Are dragons real?* My head, of course, says, 'How can they be real?' For I was a scientist once (of sorts) and still harbour a little of the mindset that demands to see irrefutable proof before it can accept a belief in the unknown. Apply that mindset to the question above and it rolls out another straightforward query: *If dragons had been indigenous to the earth, if they had lived and died here as dinosaurs did, then where's the palaeontological evidence for them?* That's a pretty good stumbling block – for scientists. But I'm not a scientist now, I'm a writer. And for writers, such questions are merely the basis of a challenge. We would point to the emergence of dragon symbology in different cultures as far apart as China, Wales and the Andes and ask, *How did that come about?* For us, 'hard' evidence doesn't matter. What we find fascinating is the awe-inspiring wonder these beasts seem to engender in apparently level-headed people in every corner of the world. It's a writer's job to examine the reality question and look for reasons around the lack of bones. On our cerebral (and sometimes spiritual) digs, we come up with theories. The one I favour most is this: that dragons were never indigenous to our earth but are instead 'off-worlders'. Aliens. Extra-terrestrials. Visitors. That last word raises another huge question, one I set out to answer in this book, one that Thomas Malone did ask of me but I decided to leave between the lines of his tragic story. The question again is pretty simple. *If dragons were here, and created such an overwhelming impact among us, why did they ever leave?*

Reader, you decide.

This has been the UNICORNE Files.

Enjoy.

Chris d'Lacey
Devon, England 2016

## ACKNOWLEDGEMENTS

Lisa Sandell has been the star I've steered by throughout this series of books. I could not have wished for a better, more convivial editor. I still don't understand how a telephone call from America can be clearer than one from four houses along my road, but when it happens, it feels like she's right there at my shoulder, being quietly supportive in every way. What a pleasure it is to work with someone so determined to fulfil my vision of a book. The same goes for her British counterparts at Chicken House, who have faithfully anglicised the stories – still can't wrap my head around that. But thank you all, anyway. I will make it to another Big Breakfast one day, if I can keep my teeth intact.

I never seem to thank the sales and PR people whose efforts have bought me a house by the sea and allowed me to indulge my passion for cars. And books would never look so beautiful or read so well if it wasn't for the designers and the copy-editors and all the work they do in the background. Thank you, guys. I do appreciate it.

Must add a quick word, too, for Natasha Farrant and her knowledge of French GPS systems. *Merci*. At last I have proof that sales conference dinners are worthwhile.

Finally, as always, I'm ever grateful to my wife, Jay, my greatest critic, my biggest ally. Quite simply, where would I be without you? Lost in the literary multiverse, I guess.

## ABOUT THE AUTHOR

CHRIS D'LACEY is the author of several highly acclaimed books, including the first two books in the UNICORNE Files, *A Dark Inheritance* and *Alexander's Army*, as well as the *New York Times* bestselling Last Dragon Chronicles: *The Fire Within*, *Icefire*, *Fire Star*, *The Fire Eternal*, *Dark Fire*, *Fire World* and *The Fire Ascending*. Additionally, he is the author of the middle-grade series The Dragons of Wayward Crescent, and the co-author of *Rain & Fire*. He lives in Devon, England, with his wife, where he is at work on his next book.

Learn more about Chris and the UNICORNE Files at www.chickenhousebooks.com/authors/chris-dlacey/.